FROM the GRAVE

by Cynthia Reeg

First Edition
First Printing, 2016

Jolly Fish Press, an imprint of North Star Editions, Inc.

Jolly Fish Press
North Star Editions, Inc.
2297 Waters Drive
Mendota Heights, MN 55120
www.jollyfishpress.com

Printed in the United States of America

THIS TITLE IS ALSO AVAILABLE AS AN EBOOK.

ISBN 978-1-631630-94-1

Library of Congress Control Number: 2016949887

To Sam and Max, my two precious mini-monsters—I love you more than sludge noodles and gravy!

FROM the GRAVE

by Cynthia Reeg

MONSTER or DIE 1

JOLLY
FISH
PRESS
Mendota Heights, Minnesota

CHAPTER ONE

Monster Rule #9: A monster's appearance should incite fear and significant revulsion to scare the socks off mere humans.

FRANK'S TALE

Moanday morning, with all its determined drear, crept up on me with silent, somber feet. It settled heavy on my broad shoulders while I waited for the Odd Monsters Out bus to arrive. Bony skeleton trees clattered in the Uggarland wind. The swirling gust stirred up a powerful aroma of decay and dread. A scent I should have relished.

I shuffled my bucket-sized feet in my freshly polished boots. Even Uggarland's gray gloom couldn't quite calm me. I sensed trouble.

Last night when I'd peeked out my cobwebbed window to spy on the demons, I'd seen a bat flying upside down. A bad omen for sure. I had a keen sense for trouble—perhaps because I seemed to be in it so often or perhaps because a bit of Granny Bubbie's witchy magic coursed through my misfit hide.

I'd heard the Demon Hours descend, louder and more terrifying than ever. That was when all wickedness ran amok in

Uggarland. The wild ones—the untamed monsters who were unable to control their antisocial ways—had free roam. Their howls and growls still echoed in my ears.

"Trouble," I muttered, as a whirl of wheels pulled my eyes to the corner. A small bus sped past the Godzilla Heights sub-division sign and screeched to a stop in front of my house. Tramping up the steps, I took a quick glance in the bus window to make sure my hair was still neat. I slammed my itchy right hand against the door and shuffled inside.

"Morning, Frank," said Mr. Aldolfo, our werewolf bus driver. He also doubled as the school janitor. Of course, he was a mis-fit like the rest of us on the crowded bus. His pink skin grew absolutely no fur—not even when the two half moons joined into one each month. As I passed, he adjusted the cap and gloves he wore to hide his smooth skin. I sighed, tugging on my long sleeves. They helped cover my abnormal blue skin. Perhaps I should invest in gloves as well.

"Hey, Mr. Aldolfo," I mumbled back.

A grinning gargoyle head popped up from behind the first seat back, followed by an even goofier grinning head. Sharp beak-like noses and bulging eyes were mirrored in the two heads attached to one disjointed body. Fifth graders Stan and Dan waved their gangly arms in the air.

"Frank! Frank!" they echoed. "We've got a new joke."

I rubbed a neck bolt. Monsters shouldn't be telling jokes. Humor was not a desired monster quality. Neither were a crisp button-down shirt and shiny shoes—as my pap had loudly re-minded me again this morning.

"Do you know what pants ghosts like to wear?" asked Dan.

Not even waiting for a reply from me, Stan answered the question. "Boo jeans!" The twins collapsed in the seat, rocking with laughter. "Get it? Boo jeans!"

"Oh, I get it." Both my neck bolts throbbed. "I just hope the two of you don't 'get it' for telling jokes like that."

"No worries," said Dan.

"Our jokes are so bad they're good," said Stan.

"No, he means, they're so good they're bad," said Dan.

"No, no. I'm right," said Stan.

"No! I'm right," said Dan. And with that their two fists started flying at each other's head.

"Settle it down, boys," said Mr. Aldolfo with a low growl. "No playtime antics on the bus." As if to drive home his warning, he slammed his foot down on the gas pedal. The bus lurched forward.

I grabbed a seat back on either side of the aisle to steady myself. "Ooops!" I cried, clomping down on Georgina's long, green, spiky tail.

"Ouch!" Georgina gurgled in surprise and sprayed me with a gush of water.

I tried to dodge, but due to my Frankenstein bulk and the small space, I totally failed. The spray splashed down the front of my neat ensemble.

"Sorry," said Georgina, pulling in her tail and wiping up her wet snout. "You startled me." Georgina, a dragon, could only spray a hefty dose of water—not a flick of fire. Not too scary of a weapon when going on a Scare Patrol to root out humans. But I suppose she might intimidate creatures who feared water would wash away their monsterliness. I'd had my hands in sudsy water way too many times to believe that old tale.

My freshly messed-up attire totally rattled my neat freak brain. But I clenched my big blue fists, took a deep barrel-chested breath, and replied, "My bad." We misfits all knew what it meant to unintentionally mess things up.

I scooted in my now squishy shoes, past several more rows

jammed with abnormal students of all ages. Our Odd Monsters Out class was a mishmash of grade levels. Age didn't matter—only oddness. With a huff, I plopped down beside my best friend, Oliver.

"Here," he said, handing me a large pile of mummy wrappings heaped at his side. "Use these to dry off. At least they're good for that."

With a fistful of Oliver's loose linens, I mopped up as best I could. I pushed down the window to let the murky air help dry my damp clothes. I frowned. There wasn't much crispness left in my button-down shirt.

"Sorry," I said. "Your wrappings are going to be soggy now too."

Oliver shrugged. "Hang them out the window to dry, until I have to put them back on."

I nodded and let a loose end stream out the window. Before I realized what was happening, the pile of wrappings at Oliver's side quickly unraveled. It flapped wildly outside the bus.

Luckily, the very end caught on the window ledge.

"Whoa!" I cried, reaching out with my long arm just in time to grab hold before it sailed away. "That was close." I reeled the strip back up into a neat ball.

"Oh, I wouldn't have minded if it all blew away," said Oliver. "Much easier to move without them."

"I know, but you'd be in dungeon detention for sure if you showed up half-wrapped." I tucked the damp roll of wrappings at his side, remembering a time long ago when a very young Oliver, free of most of his wraps, had leaped and ran and danced circles around me. A tightly bound Oliver—on the other claw—usually staggered behind me. He could hardly keep up, even when I took slow steps.

"At least I'll have more time to read in detention." Oliver pulled out a book.

"Hey, you don't happen to have one on bats, do you? I saw a bat flying upside down last night. That's got to mean trouble."

In a flash, Oliver closed up the book in his hand and pulled out another tattered manuscript from his backpack.

His unwrapped, wrinkled brown finger skimmed down the page. The low rumble of voices from the other eccentric students on our bus seemed to echo the word *trouble*.

"Maybe its echolocation powers were just damaged." Oliver pointed to the bold print.

I shook my head. "No. I think it's a message from my granny."

"Ah, your granny is gone, Frank. Remember?"

"I'm not crazy, Oliver. I was there when she crashed her broom into the tree." I blinked, still feeling Granny Bubbie's final grip on my right hand four years ago. "But she sometimes used bats to send messages."

"Upside-down bats?" Oliver said, carefully closing the book. "Well you knew her best, I guess."

"Yeah." I sniffled and rubbed my itchy right hand across my large nose. My palm burned like a poison nettlewart rash had sprouted there, but I suspected magic. Granny Bubbie's magic from the grave.

The bus rumbled on. I pulled my forbidden comb out, smoothed down my windblown hair, then slipped the comb into my pocket. "This morning, Pap laid into me again about shaping up. Looking more like a monster."

Oliver shrugged. "That's pretty typical for Moandays, isn't it? Start the week out right and keep it that way, they say. No more misfit stuff, or else."

"But Pap said he heard something big is coming down. About us."

"They're always saying that, but we manage to keep on keeping on." Oliver gathered up his loose wrappings. "You're gonna worry yourself to death."

"Only if I'm lucky," I muttered. Our special O.M.O. bus skidded to a stop in front of Fiendful Fiends Academy. The weathered engraving above the school drawbridge boasted, "Shaping monster minds for millonions."

We all climbed out. I stopped in mid-step. My neck bolts throbbed. I stiffened.

Trouble! Without a doubt. I motioned to Oliver and all the others from our bus. As misfits, we were used to being on the lookout for trouble. Being on the alert. Taking silent steps.

A moat circled the outer wall in a ring of moldy green. It oozed with a more than ample stench and unknown inhabitants. In a monster huddle, we crept toward the school.

"Wait," I hissed.

Crossing the drawbridge, I took two muffled steps and peeked inside the ancient stone archway.

"See anything?" whispered seventh-grader Vanya Kapazek, creeping behind me in her shiny white, knee-high boots. Her forbidden flowery perfume tickled my nostrils.

"Shhh," I hissed, glancing back into her single Ogre eye. Her sparkly eye shadow nearly blinded me. After one last look into the courtyard, I finally allowed myself to exhale. It was just the usual jumble of monster students scurrying into school.

An eighth grade slobapottamus dragged her mud-encrusted backpack along the uneven courtyard stones, bump, bump, bumping it behind her. A cloud of dirt swirled in her wake. A third grade gremlin's tattered trousers revealed patches of green, scaly skin. His boots trailed blobs of slime. Two fifth grade vampires sported blood-splattered shirts and spiky hair. Their frayed capes flapped about them. All were in fine monster form—unlike us.

"First gong must have rung," I said, patting the hidden comb in my pocket. Mr. Aldolfo must have mistimed the bus route again. After all, he was a misfit too.

"We'd better try to sneak in before Principal Snaggle makes his rounds," said Georgina with a gurgle. I ducked in case she sprayed me by mistake again.

"Ms. Hagmire will hang us from the ceiling if we cause her more trouble with Snaggle," said Vanya, covering her sparkly tiara with the hood of her cape.

"Here," said Oliver. "Can you help wrap me up quick? You'd better untuck your shirt and mess yourself up a bit more."

"Yeah," whispered Stan, "lucky for you Georgina doused you good already."

"Yeah," echoed Dan.

"Lucky me." With a grunt of protest, I grabbed an end of Oliver's unwound mummy wrappings and spun it about his head. "You should've done this on the bus."

"Sorry. Sort of forgot."

"Or just didn't want to remember is more like it," I muttered, wishing all the while that my best friend could have the freedom he longed for.

And that's when I heard it.

Pit-pat. Pit-pat.

I dropped the tangled strip and jerked back from the archway. Or at least I tried to pull back.

Not in time.

A claw dug into my shoulder.

"Monster Gordon," said Principal Snaggle through clenched teeth. He loomed over me. The tips of his furry sabertooth ears almost touched the arch of crumbling stone. "You seem to have overlooked several dress code requirements. Again." His saber-shaped teeth were so close to my neck I could almost feel their razor edge.

I shrugged my shoulders. For the past eleven years, I'd managed to do a fairly good job of pretending that none of the uproar about my differences mattered. But now the sweat pooled beneath my arms. I clenched my toes in my squishy boots to stop from shaking. I rolled my eyes to signal the others to run for it.

But they stood motionless, frozen like iced yuckledrops.

I had no choice—not if I wanted to give the others a second escape chance. So with a quivering hand, I slipped my forbidden comb from my pocket. There was no pretending then. I knew I sealed my doom. I took a practiced swipe and smoothed down my wet black hair. I tried to speak in the deepest voice a sixth grade Frankenstein could, but my words sounded more like a first grade goblin's squeak.

"I've got a reputation to maintain," I said loudly.

With that, the rest of my straggling classmates finally took their cue and scurried into school. That much of my impromptu plan had worked at least.

"Enough!" shouted Principal Snaggle. With one strong swipe of his claw, he spun me around like I was no more than one of Oliver's flimsy wraps. He held me by my stiffly starched shirt collar and forced me down to the water's edge. My head dangled precariously over the moat. I hardly dared to breathe for fear of falling into the murky water. Who knew what lurked there? And what was even worse, monsters—except for swamp monsters—didn't know how to swim.

"Frankenstein Frightface Gordon, you are a nuisance as well as a misfit. A decidedly undesirable combination." Principal Snaggle bent me still lower. My face nearly touched the slimy moat scum. I flung my arms behind me, scrambling for a hold but clutching only air.

"Look," he demanded, raking his free claw through the moat water. A fresh batch of piranhas popped up like overheated beezle bugs bouncing from my Granny Bubbie's frying pan. He speared two with a furry paw then spun me around. I clutched at the splintered bridge boards.

"Extreme overachievers these," said Principal Snaggle. He

dangled the piranhas before me. With fins flapping, they lunged toward my not-so-tiny nose. Their chiseled teeth tapped out a hunger-crazed tune I didn't care to hear.

"Look at their resolve." Principal Snaggle held the piranhas even closer. "Fish out of water. Yet resolute in reaching their goal. So should you be."

I tried to dig my heels in and push away. If only my boots had been properly mucked up, I might have succeeded. Instead, I slipped and pushed myself back closer toward the edge and to my fishy demise.

"Are you ready," asked Snaggle with a snarl, "to head to class and learn to be a true monster? Before something unfortunate occurs here."

Three larger piranhas leaped from the water below. Their sharp teeth snapped at the back of my neck. I tried to dodge but lost more ground, drawing another inch closer to my watery grave.

"You wouldn't really let that happen," I cried, digging my neatly trimmed nails into the rickety bridge. My fingers were quickly losing their grip. "I mean, what would you tell my parents?"

Principal Snaggle's lips curled up. "The truth, of course. 'Your son had an accident at school.' And you can guess what they would say, 'It's probably for the best.'"

I gulped. Had I disobeyed Mam and Pap one time too many, flaunting my odd attire and blue skin? What had Principal Snaggle said the last time he'd reprimanded me— "Blue skin like yours. It's unnatural. Bright as a Moratorium morning sky. Skin like that can't belong to a monster—only a mutant. Monsters are shaggy and scary. Gruesome and green. Browns and oranges and in-between. Not blue!"

The tips of Principal Snaggles' long whiskers brushed across my chin. I shuddered.

"Monsters do not have combed hair." He shuffled his large paw across my head. "Monsters pride themselves on an adequate disarray to alarm a human opponent." Principal Snaggle jerked me from the moat's edge and ripped my damp but mostly still tidy shirt in the process. He scooped up a pawful of scum as he released me and splashed the pungent green slime all over me. "And monsters should smell more like a stinkapotamus fart—not a bubble bath factory!"

"Ahhh. No! No!" I fell back onto the drawbridge, splinters gouging into my behind.

Principal Snaggle shook his head. "It's only Moanday and already I've had my fill of you, Gordon! If you want to make it to Frightday, there will be no more waywardness. Do you understand?"

I pushed myself up, not daring to look into Principal Snaggle's yellow eyes. I had to fight the desire to brush myself off and pat down my hair. Instead, I kept my big blue hands clenched at my sides and my blue eyes glued on my not-so-shiny-anymore boots.

That's when a familiar clip-clop of hooves sounded in my ear. "Wow, Principal Snaggle, sir, that was awesome! An example like that should be in our Monster Tactics Manual."

I groaned. No need to look behind me to know whose voice that was.

Malcolm McNastee.

"I could rough him up some more before I take him back to class if you want." Malcolm huffed bad breath down my neck. His overpowering troll aroma—similar to an overflowing out-house mixed with amplified B.O.—always nearly slayed me. I turned my head even farther away.

His grimy brown claw grabbed hold of my slime-drenched shirt collar. I didn't need to see his warty orange face to know it wore a triumphant smirk.

"Monster Gordon is not here for your own amusement, McNastee. He'll receive more than his fair share of harassment from his teacher. Just drag him back to class." Principal Snaggle flicked his long tail and turned to leave.

"Sir?" Malcolm's usually taunting voice sounded almost simpering. I tried to twist around, but he held me tight.

"What now, McNastee?" Principal Snaggle growled. "I've a school to run. No time to be swapping horror stories with a seventh grade troll."

"No, sir. Principal Snaggle, sir. I have . . . I mean your secretary gave me this bulletin for you. She said it was important."

Malcolm finally let go of his death grip on me. He reached inside his black leather vest and handed the principal a piece of paper.

Principal Snaggle fanned the paper in Malcolm's face. "This feels decidedly damp. Were you carrying this bulletin stuffed under your sweaty armpit?"

I cringed. My revulsion for this comely monster feature was chalked up as another misfit trait.

"Yes, sir. I was. And I'm sure it is," said Malcolm.

"Excellent, McNastee. Just checking."

I shook my head as I watched Malcolm's beaming, bumpy face. What a suck up!

"Hmmmmm . . ." Principal Snaggle's furry brows arched high as he read the bulletin. The corner of his mouth twisted up in a stilted smile. "Newly-elected President Vladimir is certainly wasting no time putting his campaign promises into practice. And I believe Uggarland will be the more fiendish for it."

"Do you really think so, sir?" asked Malcolm. "That would be something to howl about." Malcolm tossed back his head. "Hooooowwwwrrrrooooo!"

"Not now, McNastee." Principal Snaggle pushed past Malcolm. "Mayhem when appropriate. Escort Monster Gordon back to class and inform Ms. Hagmire that I need to see her later this morning."

With a flick of his tail, Principal Snaggle slunk into the shadows. Malcolm grunted and jammed his knee into my back.

"Move it!" Malcolm shoved me toward the open school door. I limped down the deserted hallway. It smelled of fermented fur and the barfeteria daily special.

"Your days are numbered." Malcolm poked my ribs.

A slimy piece of cold, green moat scum slid down my spine just then. I took a deep breath—and not because of the cool, icky sensation (which any other monster would have relished). Instead, I shivered because I feared what was coming. I knew this time I couldn't—or wouldn't—be able to stop it.

My head shuddered as a burning fire raced through my blood. My usually under-control monster anger boiled over. I jammed my elbow into Malcolm's ribs. "Like you haven't told me that before!"

"Snotfargle!" Malcolm's bulging, red-rimmed eyes opened wide. He sucked in his breath—but I don't think it was only from my jab to his ribs. I bet he was as surprised by my actions as I was. He snorted and pushed me against the rough stone wall. "Don't get smart with me, mutant mucus. I'm foreseeing your future. Your very short future."

"Oh really!" I gulped for air. "So you're a witch now, huh? Aren't they the only ones who see the future?"

Malcolm's pointy hoof clipped my shin. "Trolls hate witches. You know that!" With a grunt, he shoved his knee into my stomach.

"Oooof!" My heart pounded in my chest. I'd already been slimed and abused by Principal Snaggle. Malcolm's bad breath and worse behavior were unendurable. Beezle bung! Even an easygoing monster like me had limits.

I slammed my Frankenstein-sized foot down on Malcolm's hoof. "You smell like a mold-covered swamp slug."

"Snotfargle!" Malcolm pulled away, rubbing his flattened hoof. "Flattery will get you nowhere." With a snarl, he leaped forward, lowered his head, and slammed into my midsection.

Stumbling back into the rough wall, I clutched my stomach gasping for breath.

Malcolm grunted, grabbed my arm and pushed me down the hall. "Got some bad news for you. And the others."

"Me and the others? What do you mean?" I cringed when Malcolm snorted and sprayed troll spit across my face. "You read Principal Snaggle's bulletin, didn't you?"

Malcolm snorted again. This time I dodged the spray.

"What did it say?" By this point, we stood beneath the shadowy archway leading into my classroom. Malcolm's beady eyes surveyed the hall. Not a monster stirred.

"Before I consider telling you anything," he said, "I want an answer."

I shrugged. "An answer to what? I don't know anything about anything." And that's when I saw it. A particularly annoying wrinkle Malcolm's claw had made on my once crisp shirtfront. My blood returned to simmer mode. "Rat-splat! You messed my shirt up even more."

"So sorry." Malcolm faked a frown. "I didn't mean to do you any favors, but I guess I might as well make it worth my while." Malcolm jerked my hand from the wrinkle. A jagged rip resulted.

"Booger bombs, Malcolm! Enough's enough!"

Malcolm pressed his nose up against mine. "I'll decide on that. I want to know if you saw anything out of the ordinary yesterday on Phantom Street."

"What would I be doing on Phantom Street yesterday? There's no school on Scaredays. Only Moandays through

Frightdays." I stared in dismay at my shredded shirt. One of my favorites, with sleeves long enough to cover most of my blue skin.

Malcolm grunted. "I know that. But I thought . . . I mean someone said they saw you in the school belfry."

"Hey, not me. You must have seen . . . I mean whoever told you must have seen someone else."

Malcolm punched my right shoulder. Hard. He shoved me to the classroom door. "Go on," he said.

"Wait." I pulled Malcolm's claw off the skull-shaped door-knob. "You didn't tell me what the bulletin said."

Malcolm twisted up his thick, wrinkled lips like he was ready to sink his teeth into a barbecue bone sandwich. "I wouldn't tell you anything—except I want to see you squirm. Did you know that the new president is offering you O.M.O.s some extra motivation to reform? A deadline, so to speak."

A deadline. What did he mean? Something more than a threat or a dungeon detention for contrary choices? If President Vladimir had decreed it, then it was official. Wasn't it? I patted the strange flatness of my now empty pocket. My treasured comb lay buried deep in the dank moat waters—unless the piranhas had devoured it even before it hit bottom.

"Is that what Principal Snaggle was smiling about?" I asked. Principal Snaggle did not smile about misfits.

Malcolm nodded. His slobbering lips pulled apart. He ran his pointy purple tongue across his tarnished teeth. "I can almost taste the reptile squish-kabobs at your funeral celebration."

The sweat pooled beneath my arms again. I was tired of all this mayhem. My head ached as the anger seeped from my blood. I just wanted things to stay predictable and manageable. When I walked by, most monsters looked the other way. They pretended that me and my freaky blue skin didn't exist. I could take a few snarls behind my back. I kind of liked living a quiet life. I had no desire to be a feature write-up in *The Monster Manual of Achievement.*

My shoulders slumped. Malcolm pushed me into the classroom. I didn't even try to shove him back. Instead, I stumbled into my seat beside Oliver. A few of his mummy wrappings had already loosened and lay coiled at his feet. I grimaced. Ms. Hagmire would rattle his bones if she saw him in disarray again.

But if the rumors were true, perhaps we were all about to get our bones rattled. Much more than rattled.

CHAPTER TWO

Monster Rule #35: Proceed with cunning. Objects may be different than they appear.

MALCOLM'S TALE

Mr. Wartwood, the substitute teacher, had his reptilian back to the class as I sauntered in. I'd been officially dismissed for my office duties, so no tardy slip was required. Monsters do like to abide by The Rules. It keeps things simple that way. Less thinking and more monstering, I say.

"Copy these math word problems into your workbook," said Mr. Wartwood. "These will be part of your homework assignment."

A collective groan followed the announcement. Math was not generally a monster's favorite.

Mr. Wartwood pointed a long, twisted finger to Ivan Muckberger, the slobapottamus who sat in front of me. "Read the first problem out loud," our sub said.

"M . . . m . . . me?" Folds of gray blubber jiggled as he raised his arm into the air.

I grunted and ground my charcoal pencil into a flat nub on my wooden desk. Ivan was as slow as he was jiggly.

"Yeah, you!" I hissed. Mr. Wartwood looked my way. Dingle rot! I knew we weren't allowed to badger classmates—unless given permission. Mayhem when appropriate. Still, a low growl formed at the back of my throat. I held it in check, along with a well-deserved kick to Ivan's blubbery behind. Being a monster wasn't as easy as it looked.

"If two witches," read Ivan, "can fly forty miles in twenty minutes, how many children can they scare in two hours?"

"This is a tricky question," said Mr. Wartwood. "And don't just write, 'The witches can scare as many children as they want to.' While that may well be true, I will not accept that response for an answer. You must use the monster math techniques we've discussed today to solve this problem. Factor in the wind trajectory and flight path fluctuations. This is advanced math, students. No more relying on guesswork or monster-might to do well in Uggarland these days. You will need a solid education to succeed."

Ghoulbert Gordon, sort of my best friend, was seated across the aisle to my right. He pointed his gruesomely green thumb down.

Witches! I detested them with all their trickery and warty-noses-stuck-up-in-the-air snobbiness. I cupped my mouth behind my hand. "I've got better things to do than worry about witches and wind trajectory. I don't need to know math calculations to scare the stuffing out of anyone or anything."

Mr. Wartwood whipped his tail around, his tiny eyes narrowing in on me. The substitute teacher slipped his forked tongue through his thin lips and slithered down the aisle.

I flipped open the monster math book and pasted what I hoped was a pondering look on my face. Mr. Wartwood glided to a stop.

"Any problems?" he asked.

I held out my mud-encrusted claws. "Me? No problems here."

"Excellent," said Mr. Wartwood, but he didn't exactly sound convinced. He slid back to the front of class. "Remember, everyone. I'll need to see all your calculations as well as the correct answers on your hand-in sheets."

Another collective groan bounced off the moldy classroom walls. Ghoulbert's face crunched into a mass of green wrinkles. He slouched over his math book. "One witch times twenty miles an hour," said Ghoulbert, thinking aloud. He held open his large hand and counted on his thick fingers. It was like watching a coffin cart pileup. I couldn't look away. Ghoulbert just kept counting and recounting. Getting a different answer each time.

Finally, he groaned. "I can't get this one."

So, okay. My sort-of best friend wasn't the brightest fiend at Fiendful Fiends Academy. He had more than his fair share of challenges. Namely a pathetic excuse of a monster for a brother. That mutant Frank.

What would it be like to have such a miserable creature for a brother? I know I'd never be able to endure the snide stares and nasty remarks from all the others. Was that why Ghoulbert basically steered clear of Frank? Wouldn't I do the same if my little sister Nelly was an outcast?

"Snotfargle," I cursed. Too much thinking and not enough monstering.

I jerked to attention as the gong sounded from the belfry tower high above.

"Time to go." Mr. Wartwood tapped on my shoulder. "Morning recess."

I swallowed more curses and faked a sincere sigh. "Just trying to figure out the problem."

The teacher's lips twisted upward in a half smile. "Ah, Malcolm. You are monster through and through. One of a long line of McNastee villains, tricksters, and liars."

"I try, sir."

"Quite intently, I've observed," said Mr. Wartwood. He paused as the remainder of the class shuffled through the door and out into the noisy hall. "You probably didn't know that I worked for your grandmother at the Biped Agony Department many years back. She was ever absorbed with improving innovations for human misery."

I couldn't help but puff my chest out when he talked about Grandma Ooogle. I rubbed the lucky shark's tooth she'd given me so long ago. It hung on a leather strip around my neck.

"What a sad day it was for Uggarland when . . ." Mr. Wartwood cleared his throat. "When the accident happened."

"Grandma Ooogle wouldn't have wanted it any other way." My words were spoken low but sincere. No need to lie about my grandma. "She was too brave. A common McNastee trait. I know all about how she got sucked into that human shredding machine. She volunteered even when she didn't have to." I paused. Both pain and pride mixed into my words. "She died in the line of duty. Just like my dad."

"You've much to be proud of." Mr. Wartwood softly withdrew his reptilian hand from my shoulder. "Now, I don't want you to be telling horror stories about your sub and how I made you miss your recess. Go on."

I stuffed my math book into my battered backpack and pushed open the classroom door.

"One more thing, Malcolm," said Mr. Wartwood. "Drop this attendance sheet off at the office for me."

I grunted and crunched the paper in my claw. Maybe I'd run into Principal Snaggle again and he'd see what a valuable student I was. Maybe he'd find more ways for me to assist him. I could show him what a dedicated true-blood monster I was. That little incident yesterday with Nelly and the kitty was simply a splat on the sidewalk. And what did I care if maybe Frank had seen some of it. A monster like me need only to scary on.

I plowed into the crowded hallway, my cloven hooves beating out a loud clippety-clop against the stone floor.

"Out of my way." I elbowed Newton Bumbles. Newton was one of the outcast monster students. The little creep loved playing with soap bubbles. He smelled fresh and perfumey. Made me want to retch.

"Yes, sir. Malcolm, sir," said the lemony-scented loser. He flattened himself against the rough stone wall.

I leaned close to squeeze his scrubbed throat between my claws, but took too deep a breath and gagged big time on the little mutant's super clean scent. So instead, I pinched my nostrils shut and shoved past him.

"Next time you see me coming, assume that position, scumbutt. Otherwise, I'm gonna level you. Flatter than a roadkill pancake. Understand?"

"Y . . . yes, sir. Malcolm, sir."

I trudged down the hallway, growling and kicking, shoving and cursing all the lowlife minions who got in my path. Soon I had a flattened, quivering trail of monsters who wished they'd walked another way that day.

"Great ghost goobers!" I raised my fist in the air, grunted at a skinny first grade gremlin, and pushed another from my path. I snorted and poked my head out the courtyard door. I sent a whole class of younger monsters scurrying away with a mere flick of my curly tail—just like I'd seen Principal Snaggle do.

Thankfully recess was all about mayhem—a virtual free-for-all. Almost like a juvenile version of the Demon Hours, when the most evil, untamed monsters roamed Uggarland each night. Those monsters abided by no rules. They feasted on their own kind. Demon Hour monsters took no prisoners! Even I, Malcolm McNastee, avoided the Demon Hours. But who knew, perhaps one night I'd venture into the fray and become King of the Demon Hours too!

"Eat sugar!" I yelled, throwing a curse across the courtyard for good measure. Some of the middle graders hanging from the outhouse roof scampered out of sight when they heard me. I burped contentedly.

But as I trotted once around the courtyard—surveying my domain—my monster satisfaction faded fast. All because the scene from yesterday kept clawing its way back into my mind.

"Snotfargle!" I spat the curse into a shadowed corner. Did Frank know Nelly liked mutant cats? What did it matter? Nelly was only three. She didn't know better—that's all. I pounded my leather-clad chest. She was a McNastee true-blood troll—just like me. We were tough. Brave. Monsters to the max!

Unleashing my best McNastee growl, I booted a bully ball into a crowd of huddled students. Two or three fell to the ground from the impact. Muffled yelps and groans echoed across the school courtyard. With a triumphant yip, I trotted toward the office.

Monster or die! McNastees would never do less.

CHAPTER THREE

Monster Rule #101: In a monster surprise attack, the sneakier the better—unless you can scare them to death with your approach alone.

FRANK'S TALE

The recess gong had sounded some time ago, but Ms. Hagmire refused to let us join in the mayhem.

"It's test cram time for you. No recess!" She'd pulled her lips up tight. We'd groaned and stayed glued to our seats.

Our teacher's wrath could melt a mountain into a fiery lava flow. Her usual color was a rusty brown, but swamp monsters could change hue faster than a frighthouse kaleidoscope. All of us were very aware that the brighter Ms. Hagmire's skin color, the more upset she was. Now she shone a dull shade of crimson.

I tugged on one of Oliver's loose strips and whispered, "What's she so upset about?"

Oliver shrugged. Stan and Dan stifled a giggle. Georgina gurgled.

"Everyone," she commanded, "take out your History of Monsters books." Ms. Hagmire pulled herself up to her full twelve-hoof height. She seemed upset at the lack of interest in the classroom. With each huff and puff as she walked down the aisle, she turned a brighter shade of red. By the time she'd reached my desk, her long tail glowed like a ripe jangleberry in the moonlight.

I grabbed my book and sat up straight. Not an appropriate time for any monster shenanigans. Not a time to give a wrong answer. With heads bent low, everyone was intent on skimming through the pages, hoping she didn't call on them.

Ms. Hagmire wheeled about. The tip of her tail whacked my left foot. I clamped a big blue hand over my mouth, barely holding back a gasp of pain.

"Who can tell me the two things monsters are afraid of?" asked Ms. Hagmire, squinting through her spectacles. "And give a complete answer. Or else!"

Oliver held up a loosely bandaged arm. "All monsters are frightened of fire, which can destroy them. And water which can drown them . . ."

Ms. Hagmire thumped her tail on the floor, *thump, thump, thump.* "Because?"

"Monsters can't swim," said Oliver.

Ms. Hagmire drummed her tail faster, *thumpety, thumpety, thumpety.* "Except? A complete answer. This will never do."

"Except for swamp monsters," blurted out Georgina. "They are the only monsters who enjoy water and can swim. All other monsters avoid it whenever possible. In case some of their essence washes away."

"Finally," sighed Ms. Hagmire. "Now show me you can do better on this next question, or I may have to rattle a few heads together." Swiveling her own head in a near circle, she shot an intimidating glare at us. "Who came first? Monsters or humans? This is a tricky question."

Newton Bumbles stretched and yawned. Ms. Hagmire

whacked his foot with her tail. "Did you raise your hand, Mr. Bumbles?"

"I . . . ah, didn't hear the question," stammered Newton.

Jumping in quickly to save him, I answered. "Neither. Monsters and humans were created at the same time. They've always existed side-by-side in their separate worlds. The Shadowlands divide Moratorium from Uggarland, but monsters venture through the divide sometimes."

"Why?" asked Ms. Hagmire. "Remember. Complete answer. How often do I have to tell you?"

"Because it's a monster's duty to sc . . . scare humans," said Bianca timidly. The fifth grade ghost slipped back down inside her desk to hide.

"Correct," said Ms. Hagmire, ignoring Bianca's usual shy behavior. "And because monsters have ventured into Moratorium on numerous occasions, they have stolen a number of the humans' inventions. Give me some examples."

"Electricity," said Yasmin, a fourth grade witch with a wayward artistic flair for painting flowers and sunshine.

"What else?" asked Ms. Hagmire still glaring.

"Telephones and autos," said Oliver.

"Yes," agreed Ms. Hagmire. "And what are some of the things monsters have that humans do not? The things monsters guard and cherish?"

"Magic," cried Yasmin, careful to cover up her flowery doodles.

"Two moons," said Stan.

"Yeah, sorta like us," said Dan, pointing to their two heads. "Two moons that make up one full moon on the fourth Scareday of every month."

"The complete answer," chimed in Stan, "is that in Uggarland, we have only six days in a week and four weeks in a month.

Because it takes only twenty-four days for the two half moons to join together as one."

"Hey," cried Dan, bopping Stan on the nose, "I was going to say that. It was my question."

"Don't hit me," yelled Stan, yanking on Dan's hair. "I can answer if I want to. I'm the smart one."

"No, you're not!" Dan fired a fist at Stan's chin. The two-headed gargoyle fell to the floor, arms flying.

"Enough," yelled Ms. Hagmire, pushing the gargoyle twins back into their seat. "Don't try to earn favors with me by showing off your raucous ways. Mayhem when appropriate! Now tell me what we learned last week from chapter five in our *Unsocial Studies* book."

Stan, the wart-dotted left head of the gargoyle, called out, "I know. I know. We learned about fire."

Dan, the bald, toothy right head, carried on. "Monsters and fire. The fascination and the fear."

"Touché!" said Stan. He patted Dan's back. Apparently, they had reconciled and were back to their goofy ways. "We are on fire." Both heads bowed, looking as though they expected applause.

"Enough clowning," yelled Ms. Hagmire, still a fiery red herself. "You've saved yourself a day in detention by delivering the correct answer. But don't push your luck." Her words smoldered. I sucked in my breath and sat up straighter.

With heavy steps Ms. Hagmire stomped to the board. "Number One," our teacher called out as she wrote. "Candlelight fire is good." She rapped the board in three quick slaps. "When it is controlled! Fire must always be under control. I cannot stress this enough. A watched candle is a safe candle."

"Number two," she said, again writing on the board. "Candlelight is better for monsters than electric lights."

She swirled around. "Who can tell me why?"

No one answered—not even Stan or Dan. Though I didn't think it possible, the red of Ms. Hagmire's skin glowed brighter still.

"Look," she cried, pointing above our heads at the flickering flames of the rusty candle chandelier. "Look how the flames leap and twist. Yet their light cannot eat up all of the dark. See how the gloom still lurks. See how the shadows bend and sway. Creep and stalk. It's like a dance. The age-old monster dance. The darkness ever trying to extinguish the light."

Ms. Hagmire's eyes shone like the flames above. Her large body bobbed and swayed, mirroring the candlelight's dance. Students across the room mimicked our teacher's movements. But just as the flames lulled us into a hypnotic spell, Ms. Hagmire's booming voice shook us all back awake.

"Now then. When and why—remember, a complete answer—were The Rules written?"

Georgina gurgled and wiped away some dragon drool before she spoke in a sing-song sarcastic voice. "The Rules were written to protect us. In ancient days—before most monsters knew how to read and write—there were no rules. It was like every day and every night were the Demon Hours. Every monster could and did run wild. Doing whatever they wanted. To whoever they wanted."

"Good. Good." Ms. Hagmire nodded. "The Rules were made to give life. Go on."

Oliver spoke next. "Well, the monsters were killing and frightening each other more than they were killing and frightening humans. And when a monster pox wiped out still more monsters, the ancients had to find a way to stop all the monster deaths." Oliver tugged at one of the wrappings on his head. I opened my eyes wide, willing him to stop. But he didn't. He slowly began to unwind it. He had nearly uncovered the top of his head when he spoke again. "So they started writing rules for every monster to follow. Rules to help us monster better. And rules to protect us from each other, I guess. But don't you see how The Rules are hurting us now? There's too many of them. No one can follow all of them. We need more books and ideas—not rules. So we can think for ourselves. Even the worry over water washing away a monster's essence is purely based on myth—not fact."

"How dare you question The Rules," cried Ms. Hagmire. "The Rules have kept the monster world together. Strong. They have saved us from ourselves." She tapped a charcoal pencil on Georgina's desk, even as she fixed Oliver in her icy gaze. "And don't you dare remove any more of your wrappings, Oliver Tutamut. Mummies are meant to be wrapped. At ALL times."

Ms. Hagmire pulled back her shoulders. She pushed up her spectacles and pointed at the book she held "Now. Where were we? Yes. The Demon Hours. Who can explain them? Come. Come. I need to see claws raised. You don't want me to choose, now do you?"

I raised my hand, hoping to draw Ms. Hagmire's attention from Oliver.

"Yes, Monster Gordon."

"The Demon Hours came about because even after ages and ages of rules, well . . . monsters were still monsters. I mean, some monsters needed to have free rein to go wild, or they would implode or worse, they would continue to destroy others at will."

"Exactly," said Ms. Hagmire. "The monster deaths began to climb again, I'm afraid, before the Demon Hours were instigated to relieve the stress. By allowing the untamed monsters that time to run wild, they merely succeed in killing each other. Ah, but you forgot to tell me when the Demon Hours are. An extremely important part of the complete answer!"

"From 1:33 in the darkest night until 3:33," I said, scratching my flat head. "But aren't we still killing monsters that aren't demons? When we ship them off to Exxillium."

"You!" Ms. Hagmire held a scaly claw up. It quivered. "You are fools to talk like this. It's subversive. Do you understand? The Rules keep the evil at bay. The Rules and the Demon Hours work claw in claw to preserve Uggarland. And I'll give you this one and only one reminder about the sheer terror of the Demon Hours. Never. Ever. Venture out during that time. Do you understand? It's only two hours, but you'd have less than a newt's chance in the netherworld of making it out alive. The Demon Hours unleash the untamed monsters. There are no half-hearted snarls or gnashing of teeth. No punching or pushing or squishing. There is only death and destruction. Fangs and ferocity. Blood and guts."

I held my breath when Ms. Hagmire explained it like that. I'd never spent much time thinking about the monsters who roamed the Demon Hours. Oliver had told me once they could be anyone. He'd read it in one of his banned books.

With a glance toward the classroom door, I considered exactly what that meant. A Demon Hour monster could walk about unknown in the drear of day—and none of us would be the wiser. My neck bolts throbbed.

CHAPTER FOUR

Monster Rule #73: Late to frighten and later to scare creates a monster with nary a care (i.e., a dead monster.)

FRANK'S TALE

Ms. Hagmire pointed at the four of us—Georgina, Vanya, Oliver, and me.

"You, you, you and you! Come with me. Now!"

With a stomp of her foot, she'd dismissed our class for the remainder of recess. We four, she herded down the hall, scowling and muttering the entire way to Principal Snaggle's office.

"Ratzbotchin, another lost recess!" I said beneath my breath to Oliver. "Even misfits like us might implode without our fair share of mayhem."

"Maybe that's their plan," said Oliver.

"Silence!" yelled Ms. Hagmire. She shoved us through the office doorway.

"He's waiting for you," squawked Mrs. Rottenberg, the principal's harpy assistant. She sat perched on her office chair, tapping her beak on rusty typewriter keys.

"Sit down! Sit down," commanded our teacher. "Wait here

until I talk with Principal Snaggle about a matter of importance concerning you."

Vanya opened her mouth, but Ms. Hagmire waved her claw in the air to silence her. "No questions!"

I rubbed my still itchy right palm against my messed up pants. I hadn't a clue about any of this. Here it was, less than a gloomdial's hour later since my moat encounter with Snaggle. Was he still upset about my wayward wardrobe? Considering how much he and Malcolm had destroyed my once neat attire, I looked halfway monstrous.

But why were Oliver, Vanya, and Georgina here as well? The two girls would have been in Malcolm's seventh grade class if they weren't deemed misfits. They were a year older than Oliver and me.

We all shifted uneasily in our seats as Ms. Hagmire stepped to Principal Snaggle's door. She thumped her tail against it twice, waited for the gruff reply, then entered with a whoosh. The door caught on the edge of her receding tail, drawing a small yelp from our teacher—and leaving it slightly ajar.

"Can you hear what they're saying?" asked Oliver in a whisper.

I ignored his question and instead motioned to the trail of loose wrappings on the floor. "You'd better wind those back up."

Oliver shrugged. "Too late now. Might as well enjoy my freedom for a little while."

My neck bolts throbbed remembering Oliver's antics as a young, unwrapped mummy. Running nearly naked in his linen underwear through the cemetery. Somersaulting over swamp grass, cartwheeling past tombstones, bending backwards into freshly dug graves.

He tugged to loosen more wrappings around his forehead and nose. "Sometimes it's hard to breathe—let alone move in these things. And my view of the world isn't exactly eyes wide open!"

"Blah, blah, blah." Vanya dabbed at fake tears falling from her one eye. "An Ogre like me doesn't have 20/20 vision either. Don't feel too sorry for yourself, shorty."

She pulled away her hood and adjusted her sparkly tiara, centering it above her eye. "Enough about your 'wound-up' life." Vanya twirled a finger in the air. "We've all got sad stories—especially a little sixth grader like you. Only I don't want to hear about it."

Oliver slid down in his seat, clutching a few loose ends in his lap. I leaned close to Vanya. "Hey, we don't give you trouble about your diva clothes, or your tiara, or your makeup. So lay off my friend, okay?"

Vanya shrugged her shoulders beneath her slinky, silk top, spun with bright turquoise threads and splashed with gold polka dots. "Okay, okay. Sorry, shorty. I mean, Oliver." She fluttered her fake eyelash. Her glittered eyelid sparkled, totally nixing any fright factor possibilities. How intimidating is Summer Sky Blue eye shadow with Pink Cotton Candy brow highlights? No one knew exactly how she wrangled her makeup. Most likely a black market connection.

"Frank, can you hear what's going on in there?" Georgina tried to whisper but her noisy gurgle alerted our overseer.

"Quiet," screeched Mrs. Rottenberg. She snapped back her wings and fixed her glassy, black eyes on us in a frosty stare, then resumed her typewriter pecking.

Georgina shifted uncomfortably. She was much too large to fit on the bench with the rest of us. She sat hunched on (and sort of overflowing) the chair facing us. Her long tail snaked across the walkway between. "Go on." She winked at me and nodded toward Snaggle's door. "Take a listen."

I pushed back my thick shoulders and tried to still the boom, boom, boom of my heart. My neck bolts sent a steady hum pulsing through my body. Monsters must stay one step ahead of their opponents at all times. Or die trying. I knew the others counted on me. Even though I was the youngest of our group here, I guess it was something about my Frankenstein size and guise that made them look up to me.

In case Mrs. Rottenberg was watching, I pretended to stretch. I gently pressed my size thirteen foot against Principal Snaggle's slightly ajar door. With a creak, the door crept open a few inches more.

All of us froze, waiting to see if either Mrs. Rottenberg or the principal or Ms. Hagmire heard the noise. Georgina, with her long scope-like neck, peeked through the crack from across the aisle. She held out one tiny dragon claw and gave a thumbs up.

I gulped and edged off the bench. I pressed my right ear into the door opening. Granny Bubbie had always told me I was more than monster enough, but was I monster enough to face what I was about to hear?

"You know how important our school's record is to me, don't you, Haldora?" Principal Snaggle's smooth, baritone voice carried easily. "We can't possibly refuse to meet these new compliances concerning the students in your class."

"Certainly," replied Ms. Hagmire in a snippy tone. "My record speaks for itself. No monsters left behind in my class."

"With this latest edict, the older misfits will be the first to go," said the principal. "Fiendish Fiends Academy must achieve a Top Ghoul School Award this year. And the uncooperative students under my command will not stand in our way. I'm more than a little surprised at your hesitation to follow the President's order. I detect a distinct lack of enthusiasm for helping your students become true monsters. Through and through."

Principal Snaggle paused. I could imagine him arching his

back then and flicking his tail like he always did. "There'll be no more silly stuff! No more banned books. Or clothes. Or unbecoming behavior. Or combs or makeup or water-breathing dragons!"

"But . . . but I didn't expect such a radical change to come so soon. I thought I'd have more time to . . ."

Principal Snaggle's words were as sharp as his shiny incisors. "Time, Haldora? You are out of time. As are your odd students. Time waits for no monster."

I sucked in my breath. Ms. Hagmire cleared her throat.

"This new edict will help . . ." The sound of Principal Snaggle's claws drumming on the desktop echoed into the waiting area. "Encourage them. Especially the older ones, your sixth and seventh grade students, whose time to conform is nearly up. I've always believed we babied them much too much. Don't you agree?"

"Monster is as monster does," replied Ms. Hagmire in a singsong voice.

Principal Snaggle growled triumphantly. "I knew you'd give this an enthusiastic horns and tails up."

I rubbed my forehead. What did this mean for us—the Odd Monsters Out? I felt caught between a ground rattling thunderclap and a lightning strike. Yes, I feared this lightning was going to strike much too close.

In a desperate move, I peeked through the opening. Principal Snaggle was adjusting his prized Principal of the Year trophy on his desktop, next to his deceased pet vulture, Vincent—now stuffed and standing guard. His voice boomed louder than before. "There's no choice for the misfits but to become normal monsters. No choice. The sooner they do, the better for us all."

He paused. The ever-present gloom seemed to grow gloomier but it brought me no comfort. I held my breath as the principal spoke.

"So it's all settled then," he continued. "Today's little excursion for the seventh graders from your class. Along with those two exceptionally appalling sixth graders, that Frankenstein Gordon oddbat and that pathetic excuse for a mummy. Oliver . . . ah . . . Tut . . . "

"Tutamut," said Ms. Hagmire. "His name is Oliver Tutamut, and he's quite a bright student. Just a bit unraveled at times."

"Humpf!" snorted Principal Snaggle. "Both Gordon and Tut are dire examples of young monsters headed for extinction. I fear it's already too late to save them from themselves."

My bulky bunched body lost balance then, and I nearly tumbled into the principal's office.

Ms. Hagmire's voice shook ever so slightly. "You mean Frank and Oliver are sentenced to a day on Exxillium, too? I thought the edict said only non-responsive seventh or eighth grade students. We have no eighth grade misfits in my class this year."

I drew my hand to my mouth. Ms. Hagmire had defended Oliver and me. Could the old swamp monster have a soft spot in her scaly hide?

With a flick of his paw, Principal Snaggle waved a familiar-looking piece of not-so-damp-now paper in the air. "You must have missed the fine print, Haldora. Perhaps you need your spectacles adjusted."

The principal pointed a sharp nail at the bottom of the sheet. "Blah . . . blah . . . blah . . . 'non-responsive seventh and eighth grade misfit monsters will be sent immediately to Exxillium for a day, as a warning along with any other younger misfit students the principal deems to be dire examples of dangerous mutant behavior.'"

A low moan like we'd never heard our teacher utter before drifted from the principal's office. The four of us misfits, quivering like fresh sludge noodles, locked eyes.

"Did you hear?" I asked with quivering lips. "Us. Exxillium!"

As all the blue blood in my body drained to my boots, Malcolm burst through the office door.

"You're looking especially pastel, Gordon," he growled. "Need someone to slap a little color into you? I'd be happy to help."

I didn't even try to answer. My mouth, my entire body was frozen. I slid to the floor. I could just make out the others hovering around me. I think it was Mrs. Rottenberg, flapping wildly atop her office chair, who was yelling at us to "stay seated!" But even Malcolm had his pointy ears tilted toward the open office door.

"Exxillium!" Oliver cried in horror. He'd totally unwrapped his head to hear.

Georgina clenched her spiked tail to her scaly chest. She shook her head back and forth; substantial drool leaked from her lips.

"Exxillium!" gasped Vanya. Her frosty blue-shadowed eye blinked black mascara tears.

"We're done for," I muttered.

Malcolm cackled like a looney bird. "You are so done for."

Vanya whimpered, "Whatever will I wear to my funeral?"

CHAPTER FIVE

Monster Rule #57: A rat is a rat. Don't forget!

FRANK'S TALE

Exxillium. My neck bolts throbbed. Exxillium was a sun-drenched island full of fresh air and bright blue sky. We'd all heard horror stories about it since before we could creep. Even a short visit could do a monster in, so we'd been told.

Ms. Hagmire shuffled out of Principal Snaggle's office. "Go in," she said, motioning to Malcolm. "The principal is waiting on you." Malcolm offered me an extremely offensive monster salute then sauntered into the principal's office.

"Follow me," Ms. Hagmire said to us, not even bothering to look to see if we did. Her wiry hair stood on end. Her shoulders sagged and her tail snaked limply behind her. Oliver, Georgina, and Vanya stumbled away in something of a daze. My oversized Frankenstein feet, however, remained glued to the floor.

"You heard your teacher," said Mrs. Rottenberg. "Out! I've got to fill in for Ms. Skunkton in third grade. She just went home sick. What am I going to do with twenty little monsters?" With a flurry of wings and mutterings, Mrs. Rottenberg flew down the hall.

I turned to follow, but then Snaggle's loud voice boomed into the waiting area.

"You are exactly the monster I need," he told Malcolm.

With a now perfected scrunch and squiggle, I positioned myself to peek into the cave-like office. The principal pushed Malcolm down into the same chair Ms. Hagmire had so recently vacated.

Principal Snaggle moved beside his massive desk, staring victoriously at his stuffed vulture Vincent. Was he envisioning four less misfits at Fiendful Fiends Academy?

Malcolm tip-tapped his hooves on the floor and scrunched up his short snout. He looked like he could barely stay still. Probably too excited about our misfit troubles. Annoying misfits was his favorite kind of monster mayhem, I think.

"Principal Snaggle, sir?" Malcolm leaned forward. "You said you needed me, sir?" Malcolm prodded our dazed principal with his claw. "Sir?"

"What! Oh, right." The principal stifled a yawn and flicked his tail. His whiskers twitched.

"Yes sir, Principal Snaggle. Sir?"

"Ah, well, the situation is that I've no teachers to spare to-day with half of the faculty out with coffin cough and sniffles. So I suppose you'll have to do. I mean, I need your expertise. I want you to accompany Aldolfo with the four miscreants to Exxillium."

My neck bolts sent a zing pulsing through my body with that news. I edged even closer.

Malcolm's snout hung open. "Ah, yes, sir. A free day to harass mutants. That, um, sounds swell. But, ah, will I be safe there? On an island of misfits? Under those conditions? I've heard it's . . ."

"Of course, you'll be safe." Principal Snaggle held open his paws. "Would I send you if I didn't think you could handle the horrors for one day?"

"I guess not. I mean, no, sir." Malcolm's snout scrunched tighter.

"Stay in the shadows. Keep your ears and eyes open, McNastee. Who knows what you'll come up against in Exxillium?" The principal leaned closer. "But don't worry if you lose one of Ms. Hagmire's group there. I don't actually expect you to keep too close of an eye on them, if you understand."

I knew it! Principal Snaggle meant to make the Exxillium trip a permanent excursion if possible. I'd have to be extra vigilant for all of us.

Malcolm nodded. "I understand perfectly, sir. And I know exactly which one I'd like to misplace for good."

I gulped because I knew he meant me.

"Off with you then, McNastee."

"Aye, aye, sir!" I heard Malcolm say, as I was taking a giant step toward the door. But I didn't make my escape in time.

"Hey, scumbutt!" Malcolm twisted my arm behind my back and pushed me into the hall. "Just who I was looking for. We've got an adventure ahead!"

He snickered then threw back his head and yowled like the lead vocalist in a funeral sing-along.

A QUARTER OF a gloomdial later, I sat waiting nervously with Oliver, Georgina, and Vanya on our O.M.O. bus. Malcolm stood outside, trying to hurry Mr. Aldolfo along.

I shoved my itchy right hand into my pocket. Granny Bubbie's words from so long ago spun inside my head. "You are more than monster enough! Show 'em what you got, Frankie. The good, the bad, and the dreadful."

Oliver squirmed in the seat beside me. He'd done a quick, sloppy rewrap, resulting in a number of knots. One big knot on his forehead made it look like he had sprouted a horn.

I lightly punched his shoulder. "Hey, O. It'll be all right. It's just for a day." I hadn't mentioned Principal Snaggle's plan I'd overheard.

"Is it?" Oliver fidgeted with the bump on his head, trying to flatten it. "What if this is a trick and we're getting dumped there. Forever!"

"No way! I won't let them. I mean, they couldn't do that without telling our parents."

"Maybe they already have. Maybe our parents said, 'Good riddance.'" He pinned me with a stare. His eyes were bright, black specks peeking through the gauzy layers.

My chin sunk to my chest. Could Oliver be right? He was the smart one. The one always reading books, especially banned ones. He said those were the most interesting ones. They contained so much information we were never taught in school. Stuff about ancient monster lore and even books from Moratorium, the land of the humans. Many of the human books didn't tell you how to think but they encouraged you to think all on your own, Oliver had said. No wonder they were banned in Uggarland.

A sharp tingle in my right hand caused me to jerk my head up. More words from Granny Bubbie floated through my head. "Monster is as monster does, Frankie."

Even though my legs wobbled, I pushed myself up and looked out the window. There was Malcolm, still busy harassing Mr. Aldolfo. Taking a deep breath, I motioned to the others on the bus. "Hey, they say we're misfits—and not true monsters. But my granny always told me I was monster enough. We can show them misfits have moves too. How about we start with Malcolm?"

"What do you mean?" said Vanya with a sniffle.

"Stand up for ourselves. We don't have to let him monster us all the time without . . . well . . . without monstering back. In our own special ways."

Oliver clutched the seat in front of him. "First of all, we're already in trouble. And second of all, he's Malcolm. He's double trouble. No Fiendful Fiends monster messes with Malcolm."

I smoothed down my hair. "Well, that should doubly prove we are monster enough."

Georgina gurgled. "Maybe it is time we start walking on the wild side."

I clapped my big blue hands together. "Yes, if we monster him enough, maybe he'll be the one who gets misplaced on Exxillium."

"Bad idea. Bad. Bad. Bad." Vanya pounded her head against the bus window. "Do NOT count me in."

Oliver let go of his grip on the seat back. "Maybe it's . . . um . . . like Stan and Dan say. It's such a bad idea that it's good."

"Yes!" I punched his shoulder again. This time a little too hard in my excitement.

Oliver grunted, but then he smiled. "I'm in."

"Me three," said Georgina.

"Not me," said Vanya. "You're digging your graves all by yourselves."

Before we could try to win Vanya to our side, Malcolm clumped onto the bus. Mr. Aldolfo followed.

Malcolm threw his orange arms into the air. An evil grin spread across his bumpy face. "Ready, gang! Over the moat and past the swamp to Exxillium we go! But who's gonna make it back, only Malcolm McNastee knows." With that he threw back his tuft-topped head and let out an ear-splitting hoot.

The bus lurched forward. I collapsed into the seat beside Oliver, suddenly feeling not monster enough at all.

SOON, THE BUS was bumping on its way. The familiar sights of Monster City disappeared behind us. Mr. Aldolfo turned onto a forbidden road none of us had ever been down before. The bony skeleton trees grew smaller and farther apart. The gray gloom hovered higher. With each mile it thinned and disappeared more and more. As the gloom dissolved, its weight seemed to settle on my shoulders. We were truly entering into another realm. One that I feared was filled with unimaginable horror.

Malcolm threw a splatball at the back of Vanya's ti- ara-crowned head. Then another and another. She stayed slouched against the window, her single eyeball glued to the seat back in front of her.

Malcolm grunted. "Someone seems so very sad today. Boo hoo boo!" He threw another round of even larger, slimier splats at her. One pelted her hard on the neck.

"Ow!" Vanya flipped the splatball off. She swiveled her head my way and locked her Ogre eye on me. With a sniffle, she nodded. I winked back and motioned to Oliver and Georgina.

"Boo hoo boo! Boo hoo boo!" Malcolm advanced toward Vanya, fake sobbing all the way.

He reached as far as Georgina before he stopped. "You need to be careful about leaving stuff cluttering up the aisle," he said, pointing to the dragon's tail and taking careful aim with his hoof. "You might get stomped on!"

Georgina yelped, but then she opened her mouth and drenched Malcolm with the biggest blast of water I'd ever seen her launch.

"Snotfargle!" Malcolm swirled around with a claw raised, dripping dragon drool.

"Ooops. Did I do that?" Georgina tilted her head and scrunched up her shoulders, pretending to be all innocent. "Sorry. Misfits will be misfits."

"Misfits will be covered with bruises after I'm through with ya!" Malcolm raised his claw higher and leaned close.

"Wait. It's true," I said, trying not to laugh at Malcolm's

dripping hair tuft flattened against his orange skull. "She drenched me by mistake yesterday morning on the way to school, and she's my friend."

"We all try to stay out of her way," Oliver chimed in. "Isn't that right, Vanya?"

Vanya sniffed and set her spiky crown on the seat beside her. "Uh-huh. She's taken out seven small dwarfs with a single spray."

Mr. Aldolfo floored the accelerator, jerking Malcolm onto the seat next to Vanya. Her sharp tiara jammed onto Malcolm's curly tail. He yelped.

"Hold on," said our misfit driver, issuing his warning conveniently late to do Malcolm any good. I grinned. Mr. Aldolfo's bus was often his weapon of choice in dealing with wayward monsters.

"Malcolm, take off my tiara!" cried Vanya in mock offense, muffling a giggle.

"Dingle rot!" yelled Malcolm. He twisted and turned, trying to untangle his corkscrew tail from the sparkly crown. But the more Malcolm tried to undo it, the higher he pushed it up on his tail.

"Need any help?" I asked with a snort. "Or do you want to borrow Vanya's matching earrings too?"

Georgina gurgled a watery laugh.

"A picture is worth a million words," said Oliver, clutching his sides as more of his wrappings loosened.

With a yelp and a grunt, Malcolm dropped to the aisle floor, smashing the tiara into pieces and cutting a gash in his tail as well. "You'll pay for this." He pointed a sharp claw at Vanya then swiveled to include all of us in his threat.

Mr. Aldolfo swerved into another high-speed turn. Malcolm rolled horns over tail right into the pile of Oliver's wrappings. Fiendful Fiends' most frightful student sputtered and cursed as he furiously tried to untangle himself.

When he finally tore off the last of the linens, Malcolm balled his fist. "Be careful, Aldolfo! I report back to Principal Snaggle even on you."

With his pointy ears twitching, Malcolm settled his blood red eyes on Oliver and me. I could feel Oliver shaking beside me.

"Boogers to all of you!" Malcolm spat out the words. "You goons better not mess with me." He pushed me into Oliver, squashing my friend beneath me.

I tugged Oliver out from under me, trying to smooth out his remaining wrappings.

"I'm all right," he said. We shared a smile when Malcolm's back was turned. I saluted my comrades and gave Malcolm a special monster salute, perfect for a bully like him. We might be Odd Monsters Out, but for once we'd out-monstered a McNastee!

I tucked my ripped, slimed shirt into my pants. My neck bolts throbbed. But had we truly out-monstered him, or had we only bullied Malcolm like he always did to us?

MALCOLM PLOPPED INTO the seat across the aisle from Mr. Aldolfo, only two seats ahead of Oliver and me.

"You're one of the lucky ones," said Malcolm to our bus driver. "For a mutant."

I grimaced but slid closer to hear better.

Mr. Aldolfo pulled his cap down lower. "I'm reformed, if that's what you mean. I'm not an outsider anymore. They wouldn't let me drive the bus and do the school janitor work if I was a . . . misfit."

I shuffled my Frankenstein feet when I heard Mr. Aldolfo's words.

Malcolm snorted again. "They let you drive the misfit bus is all. And take care of the school after all the students have gone home. I bet you've never been invited to a single Scare Patrol in your life."

"No time with my work duties," said Mr. Aldolfo. He hunched lower over the wheel. Some of his smooth pink skin showed beneath his cap. It almost looked like pictures of human skin we'd seen in textbooks.

"Yeah, right. Is that why you never show up at the Halloween Feast each year either?" Malcolm threw back his head and chortled. "Who would ever be caught dead hanging out with a *reformed* misfit?"

It was true. I'd never seen Mr. Aldolfo join in any monster fun. Did our bus driver ever have any fun—or was he forced to endure one lonely day after another? I squirmed watching Mr. Aldolfo grip and re-grip the steering wheel while Malcolm mocked him.

My neck bolts tightened. I knew Malcolm was picking on him to get back at us. And even though Malcolm had deserved it, I guess we shouldn't have messed with him. Not tormenting him like he did us, anyway.

Still, as long as Mr. Aldolfo was driving the bus, he knew how to put Malcolm in his place. With a bone-jarring rattle, he jammed the gear into high and floored the accelerator. Malcolm's head snapped back.

"Watch it!" he yelled, trying to right himself.

Mr. Aldolfo turned his head to the side mirror, but not before I glimpsed his grin.

The bus rounded a bend. Most of the gray sky had crept away. No more skeleton trees, only flat, rocky ground. A shimmery glow hugged the far horizon.

Malcolm tip-tapped his hooves. His pointy ears twitched. Was Malcolm excited about tormenting misfits or was he worried like us about Exxillium?

He waved his claw at our bus driver. "Hey, Aldolfo. You got a pet?"

Huh? Why was he asking a silly question like that? Why

FROM the GRAVE

would Malcolm care if Mr. Aldolfo had a pet? I leaned even closer.

Our bus driver scratched the back of his freckled neck. He seemed a bit reluctant to answer. "Ah, just a rat. I call him Lumpy."

I drew my brows up. No wonder he hadn't wanted to answer. A rat was an unusual pet, even for a misfit. A fierce Uggarland rat could finish off small animals with a single snap of its jaws. But maybe that was the only friend Mr. Aldolfo could find in Uggarland.

"What do you keep a stupid thing like that for?" Surprisingly, Malcolm's words sounded a little shaky.

Mr. Aldolfo shrugged. "Don't know. We seemed to like each other right away."

In general, rats and monsters don't mix. Rats were rats. You couldn't trust 'em. A family might let a rogue rat hang about in order to scare away a mutant cat—like the little white kitty I saw Malcolm carrying yesterday.

Although I'd denied it earlier, I had spied Malcolm from the school belfry tower on Scareday. Sometimes I went there to think. Of course, first I had to scoop up the messy bat droppings—so smelly and so slimy. But I always wore a mask and gloves and old clothes and shoes. A little alone time looking down on my world was worth the muck cleanup.

Malcolm grunted. "I heard there was a freak kitty running loose over your way on Scareday."

Mr. Aldolfo glanced at Malcolm. "Don't know what you're talking about. Such as those are best reported to the Creature Control Corporation."

"I know that." Malcolm jammed his claw into the seat, ripping an uneven trail.

My neck bolts buzzed to see Malcolm rattled with Mr. Aldolfo's answer. But why? Yesterday I figured he was most likely playing Bouncy, Bouncy Beast or some other critter torture game with the poor white thing. But even with my giant Frankenstein steps, I couldn't keep up with him. I'd lost him in the smoky dump. Knowing Malcolm, he'd most likely thrown the white fluffy kitty into a smoldering trash heap.

Malcolm burped and rubbed his pudgy belly. The bus rumbled ever closer to Exxillium. "How much farther?"

"Just past this swamp." Mr. Aldolfo pulled his cap down more.

As odd as it seemed, Malcolm fired off another question. Only I couldn't quite hear it. Was he up to something?

"Huh?" said Mr. Aldolfo, gunning the engine. "What'd you say?"

Malcolm nudged him and asked even louder. "You ever been to Exxillium?"

Mr. Aldolfo shook his head. "No way."

"You're too afraid to go there, aren't you? Afraid they wouldn't let you return to Uggarland."

Mr. Aldolfo shrugged off Malcolm's question again. Instead he mumbled something about two witches meeting us at the dock.

Malcolm sat up. "Witches! I don't trust witches. Too much magic. That's not real monstering. Principal Snaggle didn't say anything to me about witches taking us to the island." Malcolm spat against the closed window next to him. The large green glob slid slowly down. "Goober guts! Which two witches?"

"Picklepuss and Hoofenmouth," said Mr. Aldolfo, gripping the wheel tightly. The bus swerved around a sharp right turn, nearly on two wheels. Malcolm hit the floor once again, well before Mr. Aldolfo's delayed warning. "Hold on. We're running late. Don't want to keep them waiting too long. I'd rather not rile witches."

"Pus nuggets!" cursed Malcolm, pulling himself back up.

"You'd better start worrying about riling me. A blindfolded zombie could drive this bus better than you."

Mr. Aldolfo shrugged. "The witches will fly you all to the island. I'll wait here—until nightfall." He looked back over his right shoulder at Malcolm. Mr. Aldolfo's smooth pink lips curled up ever so slightly. "That is if you make it back, McNastee." With those words, he floored the accelerator once again, and Malcolm clutched the metal bar in front of him, holding on tighter than a vulture to a maggot-packed morsel. His mouth clamped tight.

Perhaps it was Malcolm's dislike of the looming witches that finally quieted him. But whatever it was, I was glad he'd stopped abusing Mr. Aldolfo.

Oliver was trembling again. I thought maybe some small talk would take his mind—and mine—off our fast-approaching destination.

I nudged him.

"Do you remember at the Slime Pit in Monster Mall last year? When Yasmin Widget was celebrating her eighth birthday? Wasn't one of the witches that Mr. Aldolfo just mentioned at that party?"

"Yeah," said Oliver. "Witch Picklepuss is Yasmin's aunt."

"Oh, yeah. I'd forgotten. Picklepuss was friends with my granny."

"You know Yasmin's art?" said Oliver. "A real flair for the . . . ah, unusual."

"You mean her artwork doesn't fit the monster mold of grim and gruesome." I'd seen some of Yasmin's bright pictures filled with sunshine and rainbows and butterflies. Only a few monster textbooks about Moratorium showed pictures of that kind of stuff. Why would a young witch like Yasmin like bright colors and strange images?

I glanced down at my blue hands and my once neat shirt. Heck, why were any of us the way we were? "You know," I said, "my Granny Bubbie used to say, 'Monster variety adds zest to the soup.'"

"Your granny would know. She made some killer soup—especially her sludge noodles and gravy goop."

I licked my lips just thinking about its slimy zest.

"But," said Oliver, "I've also seen Yasmin perform a spell or two. She's really good for a fourth grader."

"Oh yeah, didn't she help her Aunt Picklepuss? They cast a spell on Stan and Dan—each one of them did one head."

"Poof!" said Oliver, throwing his not-so-wrapped arms up in the air. "Those goofy gargoyles transformed into a two-headed toad faster than a womp worm digs a new hole."

I smiled, glad to see Oliver relaxing a little with the silly story. "Yeah," I said, to keep my friend distracted for a bit longer, "Stan and Dan were laughing their heads off when Picklepuss and Yasmin finally changed them back before the party ended."

"When aren't they laughing?" said Oliver.

"True, but I think they may have kept a few extra warts even after changing back."

"Not sure I'd volunteer for spell casting," said Oliver. "Witches can do powerful harm when they want."

"Or powerful help." As I looked out at the bright, flat horizon, I cradled my tingling right hand. I sure hoped my beloved Granny Bubbie could help me—her not-so-little-anymore Frankie Prankie—even from the grave.

CHAPTER SIX

Monster Rule #33: Mayhem is appropriate only when those in authority determine it to be so.

FRANK'S TALE

I pressed my face against the bus window as Mr. Aldolfo rounded the last turn. The thick forest of dark, weepy trees had cleared away long ago. The bus's tires slid to a stop in the sandy soil. The air smelled salty. Stink grass grew in short clumps down to a wobbly-looking dock. There was only a hint of midday gloom here. A thin streak of light hugged the horizon where the murky water met the sky.

I'd never been this distance from Monster City before. And although it was only a short bus ride away, it seemed strange to see such a different scene. How different still must Moratorium look. Now I wondered if I would ever go there and see that world for myself someday. See humans face to face. See if humans really had books with more than rules or monster facts in them—books with ideas, imaginings, and different views.

Or would my views of the monster world and beyond end with today's trip to Exxillium?

No, I wouldn't believe that. This was a scare tactic only. I was sure. When we got back, I only needed to stay messed up for a few days, to wear long sleeved shirts to cover my blueness, to throw out a growl or two. Principal Snaggle would forget about me like he usually did. I could be the same monster I always was.

A far-off crack of thunder broke the silence. I rubbed my itchy palm against my sadly grimy pants, crusted with moat scum. I shuddered looking at them.

How I wished I could be sitting on Cemetery Hill right now, surrounded by thunder and lightning, enjoying a midday break—like Granny Bubbie and I used to do.

"Hurry up! Get out, you goons. We're late." Malcolm shoved me toward the door. I threw a practice growl at him. He smirked. "Too little too late, Frankie Prankie." I gritted my teeth when he used my granny's nickname for me. He and Ghoulbert used to torment me with it all the time.

Malcolm wedged his sharp hoof into my backside and pushed. I tumbled toward the bus steps but righted myself in time to watch him yank Georgina by her tail and tug her off the seat. "Goblin goobers," he muttered, "You're a load and a half. Move it!" He grabbed Oliver's arm and flung him into the aisle, wrappings unraveling again.

"Grrrr . . . Get going, Vanya. The witches are waiting." Malcolm yanked Vanya's shiny necklace off.

"Give me that!" Vanya lurched toward Malcolm's outstretched arm. He jiggled the beads temptingly, like holding bait to entice a Glopgoo Lizard from its cave.

"You're not gonna be needing this trash no more. I'm doing you a big favor." And with those words, Malcolm jammed the necklace in his mouth, then spit-fired bead after bead out a window.

Vanya stood frozen. Her one eye blinked back frosty tears.

"Think twice next time before messing with me!" Malcolm locked his eyes on mine when he said this. I gulped. He was making us pay for our earlier pranks. Perhaps we'd not been as monsterly as we thought. We'd only succeeded in fueling Malcolm's fire.

My right hand tingled. Granny used to say, "Mind over monster." I hadn't really understood what she meant. But maybe I was starting to. There must be a better way than bullying to show we were monster enough.

"Go on then. All of you. Nothing to look at here. Move it!" Vanya didn't protest as Malcolm pushed her into the aisle. We all staggered out without so much as a snort.

Two wrinkled crones hobbled over to us when we climbed out. They didn't seem pleased. But I recognized them as ancient acquaintances of Granny. I let out a deep breath. Somehow I didn't feel quite as frightened now.

"What took ya so long?" Picklepuss's crumpled black hat sat atop her head at a wild angle. She tapped her crooked broom with long, gnarled fingers.

"We don't fly as fast as we used to," said Hoofenmouth. Her warty nose wrinkled as she spoke. "So move it or lose it, kiddos."

Malcolm grunted and stepped forward. "Malcolm McNastee. I'm in charge here. Principal Snaggle wanted me to take these creeps to Exxillium."

"A troll in charge?" Hoofenmouth spat into her hand and slicked back a stray strand of greasy, gray hair. "What's this nightmare coming to?"

Trolls and witches had a long harsh history in Uggarland. The trolls blamed the witches' magic for the terrible hoof pox of the first millonion. It had crippled and killed troll after troll. The witches blamed the trolls for an out-of-control fire at the witches' centennial—the Viletimes Jamboree in the Year of the Corpse, so long ago. In a protest, the trolls had built the biggest bonfire ever and thrown every book from the witches' spell slybrary into it. The trolls had been so crazed with hatred they'd braved even the massive inferno to rid Uggarland of witchy ways.

We'd learned in Monster History how hundreds of witches had lost their lives that night, trying to retrieve the irreplaceable tomes from the flames. The witches had fizzled in the blaze like so much tinder. Since they couldn't pass their magic on to any others, the total witchy magic was greatly diminished that night. Tragically torched—a catastrophic loss. Since then, neither species could forgive the other.

Malcolm grunted in response to Hoofenmouth's words. With his shoulders hunched and his pointy hooves posed, he looked ready to pounce or—could it be?—run away.

Picklepuss shook her broom at Hoofenmouth. "Enough, Greta. No time for squabbling now. Save that for Scareday. My instructions are to lead the way, and you will bring up the rear."

"Why am I always the rear end?"

"Takes one to know one, Greta." Picklepuss smirked, then pointed at Oliver and Vanya. "Looks like this dragon should be able to carry those two." She grabbed my arm. "I'll take this one, and you can take the troll." Picklepuss stirred up a cloud of dust as she hobbled past her partner. "That'll give you two plenty of time to get to know each other."

"Blasted bunions, Penelope. Just wait 'til it's my turn to be team captain. Then we'll see what assignments I give you."

"Witchever," said Picklepuss with a shrug. "Don't wear out your wattle, Gretta. Save your meanness for when it matters. It's time to fly."

I couldn't help but grin. The two reminded me of Granny and her grouchy, witchy ways.

Oliver stood quaking at my side. I picked up a loose strip trailing behind him. "Um, Witch Picklepuss, would it be okay for my friend to ride on your broom too?"

Picklepuss flapped her hat before her reddened face. "Look at me. I'm already overheating and we haven't even taken to the skies. You're no lightweight, Frankie. And now you want me to add more cargo."

I was surprised she'd remembered me. "If you could. Please."

"Blasted bunions! Don't go getting all snivelly on me or I'll make you swim to Exxillium. Come on—the both of you."

I threw my leg over Picklepuss's broom. It was like old times with Granny Bubbie. Oliver crawled behind me. He was still shaking. "Hold tight," I said. "It'll be okay. Just don't look down." Vanya climbed on Georgina's broad back. Her scaly wings began to beat. Malcolm seemed reluctant to join the group.

"Saddle up, troll boy," said Hoofenmouth. "And don't expect me to catch you if you fall."

I swear Malcolm's claws shook more than slightly as they wrapped around the rough broom handle. I grinned again. Malcolm—brave, monsterly Malcolm—was afraid to fly. Or could he not endure being so close to a witch?

With a throaty cackle, Picklepuss shot us into the sky.

"Hold on tight, boys. I'm kicking it into high gear."

My stomach dropped to my toes. I tucked my head behind Penelope Picklepuss's giant hat. Oliver gasped. For once, he should have covered his eyes with his wrappings. "Remember," I yelled back, "don't look down."

The salty sea wind blew cool against my ears. My recently tattered shirt snapped against my behind. I thought I heard it rip still more. I cringed.

"You remembered me." I shouted the words into Picklepuss's hat brim. I hadn't seen her since Granny Bubbie's funeral four years ago. I was quite a bit bigger and bulkier and bluer now.

"Warts and wood toads! Of course, I remember my best

friend's favorite grandson. Helzabub always had a new picture of you floating about in her crystal ball."

My heart flip-flopped when she said that. I blinked back tears. Granny Bubbie seemed so far away.

Picklepuss accelerated and we climbed even higher. Oliver's grip around my waist tightened. I clenched the knotty broom handle. I could understand why Malcolm was so terrified. But still I forced my eyes wide open, imagining what Granny saw when she sailed the skies. How she loved to soar and swoop. To the very end—to the day of her tragic accident.

The ancient skeleton tree had towered on the edge of Granny Bubbie's yard. As a silly seven-year-old, I always imagined the tree as an outstretched claw. I believed that tree reached up and up, into the eternal gloom of the monster kingdom's sky. Holding it fast. And I knew that one day, when I was big enough, agile enough to climb all the way to its tip-top, most fragile, bony branch, I'd be able to clutch a handful of Uggarland too. I'd grip it tight, keep it steady, and never let it go. Uggarland and me would be one.

At least, that was the unspoken pact between me and the tree before the crash. Granny Bubbie's final crash. Her final crash on her magic broom. The crash I caused.

Waving my seven-year-old arms above my head and shouting in Frankenstein mega-mode, I'd morphed into a ghastly distraction for any incoming air traveler. Especially my ancient, near-sighted granny.

"Don't be mad at me, Granny! Ghoulbert made me do it!" I yelled up at her from the ground below. She circled overhead, trying to align her rather out-of-control landing. The giant skeleton tree watched silently by my side.

"I didn't mean to hurt his silly spider," I blubbered. "Didn't mean to. Didn't mean to." I jumped up and down, pounding my chest, ripping at my hair. Screaming like a ghost caught in a vapor trap.

Granny dipped and dived. She veered and vaulted. She nearly flew upside down.

"I'm coming, Frankie," she called. "As fast as I can." But then her hat flipped off. A witch's hat is an essential part of her attire. No two are exactly the same. Granny's was covered with honor badges from years of Viletimes Jamboree gatherings. Trying desperately to snatch back her hat, Granny took her hands off her broom and totally lost control.

"Granny, watch out!" I cried. But my warnings were too late. I'd already disrupted her return flight with my horrific tantrum display. This was long before I'd better learned to lock up my monster anger. Well, unless Malcolm was involved.

Splat went Granny into the claw-like tree beside her house. I screamed and dropped to her side. She lay sprawled at odd angles. Her hatless gray hair fanned around her wrinkled green face. She fumbled for my hand.

Granny wheezed and sputtered. "I didn't see that bony tree jump out in front of me. I was aiming for my open bedroom window." That was half-a-house away.

"Now would be a good time for your magic, Granny."

Her nearly toothless mouth creased into a crooked grin. "This is even more than my magic can fix, Frankie."

A startling heat surged from her cold fingers. I yelped as it singed my right palm.

"There," she said. "The last of my magic."

"What do you mean?" I tugged on her torn sleeve. I pumped her limp hand. "Let me go get help. One of the other witches will be able to put you back together again. I'm sorry I messed up your flight. You lost sight of the window."

"Too late for any help, Frankie Prankie." Granny's eyes held me like a hug. "And don't you dare think I crashed 'cause of you. My silly goggles steamed up. That's all."

No matter what she said, I knew she was only making excuses. I hiccupped a giant sob.

"A witch can muddle through only so many crashes in a lifetime."

"No, Granny. No! You can't leave me."

"I won't," she said. "I'll be there when you need me."

Granny paused. Her rattling breath seemed to catch in her throat. She squeezed my hand one last time. "Don't you dare let them make you into what you don't want to be. You are more than monster enough."

I swear I heard the tree sigh then. I pressed my forehead against its cold, hard bark. Its chill encased me like a tomb.

"I promise, Granny. I promise. I'll be my own monster. I'll be monster enough. Just don't leave me. Don't go!"

I'm not sure that she heard my words though; Granny Bubbie breathed no more.

Now I blinked at the brightening sky. The freshening air burned in my nostrils. No more time for rememberings.

Uggarland's few lingering clouds were quickly falling behind us as we raced ahead. I ducked even lower beneath Witch Picklepuss's black brim as the sky lightened and warm rays beat down on us. The soggy, stale monsterland air thinned. My nose tickled with each breath of the strange fresh atmosphere.

"You okay back there?" I called to Oliver.

"For now," he croaked, multiple loose wrappings flip-flapping about him.

"The noxious gases are awfully thin out here," yelled Witch Picklepuss. "Let me know if you need a whiff of this." She waved a green, crusty rag toward me. The aroma of swamp muck swept up my nostrils. I jerked my head back as a burst of energy zipped through my innards.

FROM the GRAVE

I certainly didn't delight in the strong aroma like a monster should, but I was surprised how much the mucky air refreshed me. How did a monster live without foul air? Could a monster, even a misfit monster, survive long without it?

I leaned left and peered around Witch Picklepuss's skinny form. A dot of green gleamed amid the sparkling blue waters. The intense reflections from the waters bounced up and all around. I narrowed my eyes. I'd never seen so much light. It sparkled brighter than if all the candles in Uggarland had been lit at the same time.

"Here. Put these on." Witch Picklepuss passed back a dented pair of goggles. "I always try to keep a spare pair since your granny's disaster. A prudent witch is a prolonged witch, I say."

I knew that even with an extra pair of goggles, Granny Bubbie still wouldn't have survived my distracting display. Sighing, I passed the goggles back to Oliver. "Thanks but I'll never get these around my big head."

As long as I stayed beneath the witch's hat, I could deal with the glare. The island grew larger and the tall swaying trees bordering the white sand beaches grew greener. As we drew close, I spied a group of monsters dotting the beach. It was either our welcoming party or a disgruntled pack of outcasts ready to take their revenge on us.

I looked back. Georgina's strong wings flapped so fast they were a blur of green. Vanya hunched low on her back. Malcolm was swallowed up in Witch Hoofenmouth's streaming black cape. I could only catch intermittent glimpses of his clenched claws and bumpy head. But I heard numerous groans and curses from the grouchy troll loud and clear.

Too soon for me, Witch Picklepuss steered her broom down. We shot toward the beach like a vulture plunging toward its next meal. My stomach jammed into my throat and threatened to keep going.

Oliver moaned loudly and nearly cut off my air supply with his grip about my waist. I gulped and squeezed my eyes almost shut. I wasn't sure I wanted to see how this witch landed—or crash-landed—her broom.

"Whooooeeee!" shouted Witch Picklepuss. "I was born to fly."

I heard Witch Hoofenmouth echo the cry. Georgina, too, whooped a triumphant dragon roar. I'd never heard her sound as excited as that in school. Not even during our monster growl classes.

"Either tuck your oversized feet up," Witch Picklepuss shouted back to me, "or use them to help slow us down. My brakes need some fine tuning."

I dropped a few choice phrases myself and wrapped my not-at-all-polished black boots beneath my butt. Oliver tucked his toes up as well. At the speed we were flying, I'd be minus both feet if I attempted to stop this broom. I tried to focus on the only good thing that could come about if we did crash land—I wouldn't have to ride another broomstick with Witch Picklepuss ever again.

"Make way for monsters! We're coming through." Witch Picklepuss cut a zigzag path through the exiles gathered on shore. They dropped and dodged from our path. Our momentum slowed only slightly as we shot toward a long thatched hut.

"Whooaaa!" I yelled as we narrowly zagged past.

We skimmed a mound of tall grass. "Yecccck!" I was almost too busy spitting out a mouthful of green to see we were headed straight into a pile of black.

"Watch out!" cried Oliver.

"Ooooooof!" I tumbled off the broom, rolled blue head over heels, and lay sprawled in something potent and slimy.

"There. We did find a soft landing," said Witch Picklepuss, brushing bat droppings from her hat. "Without me even needing to use a spell. Why waste a perfectly good spell, I say. Waste not—witch longer."

"Pfffft!!!" I snorted bat poop out of my nose. Oliver, nearly a third unraveled by the wind, leaped from the broom. He nearly landed on his feet but, instead, tumbled into the slimefest. I knew if his legs weren't still wrapped so tightly, he'd have stuck the dismount easy. I snorted out more bat poop and yanked him out. His bandages were now a smelly shade of brown.

"Frank, I can't believe it. We made it." Oliver fished lines of his loose linen from the bat poop pit.

I muttered a weak, "Monster on," and bumped my big blue fist against his, then collapsed onto a rough wooden bench nearby.

Oliver pulled the last of his wrappings from the pit. "Hey, I'm going to step down to the beach and see if I can wash any of this off. Even Principal Snaggle would think this amount of slime is overkill."

"Yeah, me too." I stomped sand from my boots, holding my arms outstretched to avoid further poop smearage on my clothes.

"Wait." Witch Picklepuss blocked my path with her broom. "I want to talk to you."

"Go on, Oliver. I'll be right there." Then I remembered Principal Snaggle's advice to Malcolm on losing as many of us as possible. "Just stay close though," I called after him. I watched Oliver waddle to the tide while giant fruit bats squealed from the branches above. They seemed none too happy to have their naps disrupted.

"You okay, Frankie?" Witch Picklepuss tilted my chin up toward her gray face. "You're looking kind of pale."

Great! Even when I got scared, I only turned a more pathetic pastel shade. Maybe Granny Bubbie was wrong. Maybe I wasn't monster enough. Maybe I did belong right here on Exxillium for good.

"That is not true!" cried Witch Picklepuss. She bopped the flat of my head with her broom handle. "You don't belong here. Helzabub would be rattling her bones if she knew you were ready to give up."

My mouth dropped open.

"Shut that fly trap. I've always been a quick mind reader when I needed to be. Helzabub, on the other wart, couldn't read a newt's notions—hard as she tried. Some got the gift. Some just pretend."

"But if I go back to Uggarland, that's what I'll have to do," I said. "Pretend. I'm not cut out to be a real monster. I'm not the right color. I don't want to scare humans. I don't want to use my anger to hurt a monster or a human. And I just can't stand being covered in bat poop . . ."

I paused and snorted out another nostril-full. I clutched my stomach, ready to barf from the smell. Tons more of it clung to my shirt and pants and dripped from my hair. I tried to shake myself out like a wet werewolf. But it did no good. I had to have relief. I stepped over the witch's broom, ready to splash away as much grime as possible in the salty sea.

"I'm not finished yet!" Witch Picklepuss held out her arm.

ZAP! My body froze in mid-step. I was suddenly a smelly, dirty, Frankenstein statue—and a captive audience.

Witch Picklepuss stomped her foot. "There. That should hold you for a bit. Now as I was trying to tell you, I remember a Halloween Feast years ago. You were probably only about five. Your neck bolts hadn't even popped out yet."

I couldn't feel my now prominent neck bolts, frozen with the rest of me. I'd forgotten when they hadn't been a part of me. That was my very first Halloween Feast. Most everyone was in a strange costume. A new color, shape, and size. Some even dressed like humans.

FROM the GRAVE

Picklepuss nodded, reading my mind. "And do you recall what you said when you saw the whole spectacle?"

Of course, my statue self couldn't shake my head to say "no," but then my right hand seemed to catch on fire. Granny's magic melted my frozenness. My arms dropped. My lifted foot touched the ground. And a scene floated before my brain. I heard my five-year-old Frankenstein voice. "Look, Granny! Nobody cares what color I am tonight. Everybody's a different color. But we're all still monsters. I wish it could be Halloween every night!"

Picklepuss nodded. "That's what I wanted you to hear again, Frank. We're all still monsters."

I clutched my hands together, staring at my pale blue skin.

Picklepuss steadied herself with one hand on her broom and one on my shoulder. "It's just like my landing. Monsters' paths are more often crooked than straight. But I don't need my crystal ball to see that right now you're aiming for disaster. At full speed. If you're ever gonna have a chance of getting to where you really want to go, you gotta believe in where you're headed first."

"Huh?" The witch's words didn't make any more sense to me than one of Granny's scribbled magic recipes. "I don't want to head anywhere. I only want to stay put. In Monster City. In Uggarland. With my family and friends. Why can't the others let us be?" I sighed from somewhere so deep inside it hurt. "If we're all still monsters."

Witch Picklepuss looked thoughtful as she repositioned her battered hat. "Maybe it's up to you to show them."

"How?"

"If you've got only a whiff of your granny's wiles in you, I'm sure you'll come up with a way. Helzabub in her prime was a witch to best the bestest." Witch Picklepuss patted my wide shoulder. "Frank, you are more than monster enough!"

I gasped when I heard her repeat Granny Bubbie's words.

The clump, clump, clump of feet drew closer. It sounded like the others were approaching our crash zone. A damp and slightly less slimy Oliver drew to my side. He still held a large pile of wrappings in his arms.

Witch Picklepuss quickly straddled her broom and hovered above me. After scanning the beach, she waved a gnarled hand in the air. "Wait up, Greta."

Her black cape sailed behind her as she flew down the island to meet her friend. I was still too numb to even nod "goodbye." Too befuddled deep down inside to understand all she meant.

"Monsters only believe in monstering," I muttered.

"Huh? What did you say?" asked Oliver.

"Nothing." Right now all I cared about was getting clean again. I grabbed a long damp strip from Oliver's pile and wiped my face and scrubbed furiously at my clothes.

A list of my odd-monster-out ways popped into my head:

My total neat-freak obsession.

My pathetic and so unmonsterly blue skin.

My quest for the quiet life.

Yet even when I truly feared that my wayward life was out-of-control, all I did was flick more bat poop off my beyond-hopeless shirt and pants.

But this was the real me! Everyone couldn't be like Malcolm—all guts and gore. Somehow I had to figure out a way to stay genuine and to stay in Uggarland, my home.

Blasted bunions! I knew it was going to be a bumpy, crooked path getting there!

CHAPTER SEVEN

Monster Rule #1: Follow the rules, or else!

MALCOLM'S TALE

From beneath a sliver of shade, I lay moaning. Even though Hoofenmouth had deposited me on the beach a short time ago, my insides remained upside down and downside up.

"Hummmf!" Hoofenmouth had said, when she'd dumped me from her broom. "Trolls. Always acting so high and mighty. Look who's a mess of a monster now."

"Booger off," was all I could manage to retort. I had to lean over and barf up my breakfast then.

Now with each breath, fresh air rolled into my nostrils, bringing new bouts of nausea. I needed to find the misfits. I needed to monster up. Fast!

Trying to take my mind off my spinning head and upset stomach, I pretended to sniff the aroma from an overflowing outhouse on a breezy day. I pretended to hear the final school gong on a Frightday afternoon. I pretended I was on a midnight stroll with countless, unknown eyes peeking through the shadows. First past the stagnant swamp, then through Cemetery Park, then into the midst of the smoldering, smelly dump.

Ah! A little relief . . . until I remembered clutching Nelly's fluffy white kitty above the trash heap last Scareday. Holding it high over the decay, ready to drop it to its death—but not doing it.

"BURP!" I nearly brought up more breakfast.

No more thoughts of bus drivers with rats big enough to eat fluffy white mutant cats in one gulp. Only thoughts of bullying misfits—broken tiaras, stomped tails, scared mummies, and squirming Franks. Better yet, no Frank at all. A forgotten Frank left on Exxillium!

"Monster or die, Frankie Prankie!"

"BURRRPPP!" Ahhh!

Much better. I pushed myself up and saw the misfits gathering at a nearby poop pit. They didn't look too great either. I grinned and trotted over.

Oliver tugged on a mishmash of wet wrappings. Frank stood at his side, obsessed with poop cleanup.

Vanya tried to tiptoe around the slimy pit, but I made sure to give her a shove. Splat! She was ankle deep in doo-doo.

"Oooh!" she squealed. "Look at my white boots. They're ruined!"

I snorted. "You can go ahead and thank me for that."

She kicked a clod of bat poop in my direction. "I hate you, Malcolm McNastee!"

Georgina slashed her tail between the two of us, flipping new sprays of bat poop all around. "Leave her alone, Malcolm. You weren't exactly the bravest monster on the ride over."

Vanya sniffed. "Or during the landing either."

Georgina nodded. "Yep, Witch Hoofenmouth really showed off her stuff with the landing."

"Zippty-zips and whoosh-arounds," said Oliver, wiggling an unwrapped brown finger through the air. "I heard your screams loud and clear."

Frank waved a big blue hand before his nose. "Yeah, and it smells like you've been barfing your guts up."

"Ha!" said Georgina with a gurgle. "Seems like trolls aren't too taken with aerodynamics."

"Need to keep your hooves on the ground, huh, Malcolm, to be monster enough?" said Frank.

"Booger off!" I said, snapping my sharp teeth at them. "Remember. I've got your tickets out of here." I opened the four talons on my right claw, one by one. I held out my empty claw. "Oops. I seem to have lost them all. Welcome home, misfits!"

Georgina gurgled. "No. That's not true. You can't leave us here!"

"Ms. Hagmire said it was just for a day!" Vanya's voice quivered. Her dangly earrings shook as well.

Oliver trembled at Frank's side. "I knew it. I just knew it."

I laughed. My tail crinkled with glee.

Dropping his rag, Frank stomped forward. "Stop messing with us, Malcolm."

I grabbed a clawful of Frank's shirt, twisting the slimy mess tight. "Then don't you mutants EVER try to mess with me again. You don't want to pay the price for making that mistake twice. Got it?"

"We got it," said Georgina.

"Ya," said Vanya.

Oliver nodded. He nudged Frank. "Tell him you got it."

"It don't matter," I said, pushing Frank down into the sand. "Frankenstein stupid-face Gordon's chances are already used up with me."

A group of island monsters was encircling us now. Probably enjoying our free-for-all fight. I eyed some of the strange creatures approaching. A bizarre purple gargoyle wore orange fruit rinds on every spike of his body, including one on the end of his nose. He fanned his face with green palm fronds, gasping for air. I shuddered. It was like a Moratorium clown gone wrong.

A shrunken hunchback crawled toward me on all fours through the sand. The creature looked more like a turtle than a monster. Flaps of dangling, sunburned skin hung from its face. I stepped quickly away, and right into the path of a skin and bones slobapottamus. He'd lost so much weight that he carried overlapping folds of his stretched-out skin in his thin arms, nearly tripping on it with each labored step.

I blinked, trying to end this vision of monster monstrosities surrounding me on all sides, but the mad mass grew even larger. Desperate cries and groans and a chilling laughter filled my ears.

Was I the only true-blood monster on this cursed island? What atrocity would a true-blood have to commit to be sent here? I snorted. No real monster would ever commit an act that would land him on this hideous island. For that at least, I was glad.

"Greetings!"

I spun around. A bright-eyed creature stepped from the pack. His face sagged on one side, and his smile revealed a mouthful of missing teeth. He dragged a foot behind, leaving a distinctive trail in the sand.

"Hey," I said holding up a slightly shaky claw. "You in charge here?"

He smiled wider, showing more black holes where teeth should be. "I'm only in charge of the entertainment."

"Huh?" I snorted.

"My name is Gooney," he said with a laugh. "I'm a zombie who likes to throw zingers. Here's a good one! What's a ghost's favorite dinner?"

Nobody answered the weird question.

Gooney laughed. "Spookghetti!"

"Huh?" I said again, rubbing a claw through my spiky hair.

Was everybody here an idiot? This monster looked like a zombie, but he was way too lively. More like a gremlin after a dose of oomph juice. Zombies didn't tell jokes—even bad ones. They could barely hold their glassy eyes open and moan at the same time. This Gooney reminded me of those imbecile gargoyle twins, Stan and Dan. For sure they'd end up here. Perfect company for this jokester.

"Hey! Where's the guards?" I yelled desperately. "Anybody here to take charge of these misfits I brought today?"

I dug a hoof into the sand. The queasiness in my stomach suddenly threatening to return. What if we'd ALL been dumped on Exxillium with no hope of return? Principal Snaggle would never do that to me, his loyal follower, would he? With a slightly trembling claw, I yanked on my green hair tuft. The principal couldn't possibly know about the white cat, could he?

"Wait your turn, troll." A hulking thug pushed through the crowd. He wore a breastplate and helmet and carried a large double-edged broadaxe at his side. "We got a whole island to patrol. Had to clean out a cave this morning on the far side. Some mutants thought they could build a raft and exit this paradise."

"Grrr!" Another guard drew up beside the first. "We showed 'em that weren't happening."

Both Minotaurs stamped and snorted. They clinked together the chiseled edges of their axes, celebrating their earlier victory. Long, curled horns poked through their helmets. Each wore a shiny brass nose ring.

Ratzbotchin! Two real life Minotaurs! My ears stood straight with the thrill of it. The few Minotaurs that remained in Uggarland trained as combatants for the annual labyrinth duels. I'd only seen pictures of them. In fact, I had a personally autographed photo of last year's winner, Deadalus Bullfull. I'd won it at the Bobbing for Gizzards contest during the Halloween Feast. But I'd never heard about Minotaur guards on Exxillium. My tail twitched back and forth.

The bigger of the two giant monsters grabbed a scrawny young witch from the crowd and pushed Gooney out of the way.

"Here's your tour guide to this exotic isle. She hasn't been here long, but she's a fast learner. For a mutant. Ain't you, Zelda?" The Minotaur tipped up the witch's face using the end of his broadaxe. One twitch from the teen witch and her head and neck would no longer be attached.

My tail twitched. Finally, some real monstering. These two knew how to put mutants in their places. Maybe I should add some ax moves to my scare tactics.

Zelda stood fast. Her black hat drooped so low over her face that I couldn't see her eyes. Her lips, though, were drawn into a tight line. Dirty gloves encased her hands. Instead of a broom, she held a shovel.

"She ain't much of a talker," said the other Minotaur, stepping closer. "But if she don't do a good job showing you the place, just let me know. I'd be happy to teach her a lesson—one way or the other." He snorted, puffing steam from his whiskered snout.

I snorted thinking about what torture those two could devise for a wayward witch. A tug-of-war contest with the winner yanking off the biggest chunk of witch, maybe.

The first Minotaur swung his broadaxe above his head. "Clear out, the rest of you. Especially you, Gooney." He grabbed the still-grinning zombie by the shirtfront and lifted him high above the sand. "How often I gotta tell you? No more jokes!" He threw the misfit zombie down and kicked sand in his face. Gooney sputtered and crawled away.

The bigger Minotaur's voice boomed. "You, troll."

"Yes, sir. Malcolm McNastee, reporting for duty, sir."

FROM the GRAVE

He snorted. "Yeah, whatever. You can go with Zelda and the mutants on the tour, if you want. Just make sure they come back to the main hut in time for the return trip. Think you can handle that?"

"Yeah," said the second Minotaur. "We don't want more of these creeps to hunt down."

I nodded. "Yes, sir! I mean, sirs!"

"Good," said the second Minotaur. "Cause I'm hungry." He poked the bigger monster with the tip of his long horn. "How 'bout we barbecue one of those misfits who tried to escape this morning. Pay 'em back for causing us so much extra trouble."

"Grrrr," growled his partner. "I do love me a barbecued mutant! Dibs on the ribs." They threw back their massive skulls and chortled, jabbing each other with the wooden handles of their axes as they stalked away.

I wrinkled up my snout. Were the Minotaurs really barbecuing misfits? Well, sure. Why not. Mayhem when appropriate. Especially mayhem for exiles trying to escape. I just hoped they enjoyed their feast downwind of me.

Zelda jammed the shovel into the sand. "Stupid Minotaurs," she muttered.

The mummy trembled next to Frank. Vanya huddled close to the drooly dragon, who had her tail clenched in her claws. Frank followed the Minotaurs with his eyes, his brows drawn close. I blinked. It must have been all the bright light in this awful place, but Frank's right hand almost seemed to glow.

"Come on," said Zelda. "Let's get this tour over with. Not that there's much to see." She scooped up a shovelful of bat poop and dropped it into her apron front. Frank cringed when she touched the bat goop. With an exasperated sigh, she gathered her apron up and waved the shovel at us. "The sooner you follow me the sooner you'll get out of here—hopefully."

Stupid witch. What did she mean by that? I snorted.

"I guess you heard," she said. "I'm Zelda. I'll show you where we eat and sleep and stuff. Then you need to find some shade before the sun gets any brighter, or you'll end up fried."

The sun beat down on us from directly overhead. My neck practically sizzled. If my nostrils weren't so overloaded with fresh air, I probably could have smelled roasted troll. Snotfargle, I'd even wear a goofy hat like Aldolfo's to keep these death rays off me.

"Luckily, I'm protected," muttered the mummy, holding out his re-wrapped arms. Frank turned up the collar on his stupid shirt. Vanya edged into his bulky Frankenstein shadow.

"I've flown places like this before," said Georgina. "It's not so bad."

"You're crazy, dragon," I said. "We're all gonna toast faster than cronkodile toes on a skewer if we don't get in some gloom soon."

We stopped in front of a long hut. Zelda motioned us to peek inside. "Go on. Take a quick look, but we can't stop for shade yet."

The sun crept into much of the hut, revealing a severe shortage of cobwebs. An abundance of leafy branches covered the floor. After inhaling two-lungsful-too-many of the fresh, tangy, sea-breezed surroundings, I snorted. "That smell is pure torture."

Vanya wrinkled up her nose, pressing a perfumed hanky against it. "Is this where everyone stays?"

I understood exactly what the glitzy Ogre was hinting at. Just being in close quarters with these mutants for half a day already made me want to slaughter them. I couldn't imagine spending the rest of my life here on this tropical abomination. But wait! My mind must be going fizzy on me. Principal Snaggle wouldn't ever leave me here. Would he?

Zelda shrugged. "There aren't many other choices. The

caves on the other side are off-limits. Sometimes one of the little gremlins or ghouls finds a rock to burrow under when they're really homesick. But you can't stay homesick for too long."

"Why?" the mummy asked with a shaky voice.

"You'll implode!" The witch's harsh words pushed us all a step back.

"Implode!" Vanya gasped. Her ugly makeup-smeared eye opened wide. We all knew what "implode" meant. Monsters suffering from prolonged emotional turmoil often burst from the internal pressure. Heck, I'd even reviewed the whole thing with the younger cadets recently in our Junior Scare Patrol unit on Casualties.

"We are finely tuned creatures," I'd read out loud, from under the heading 'Sensory Overload.' "Sometimes a mission is too intense for a monster. In this type of situation, the monster shatters into countless bits and pieces. If you encounter such an emergency, you must realize it is impossible to put this monster together again. Let the pieces fall where they may. Keep calm and scary on."

But no one had told me that a monster imbalance could happen outside of a Scare Patrol mission. How long would it take on Exxillium before bits and pieces of one or more of these Fiendful Fiends Academy misfits lay scattered on the shore?

I grunted. "Hey, Zelda. How long you been here? You don't look much older than us."

Her muttered words were nearly swallowed up in the incessantly fresh, salty breeze. "More than long enough."

"You said it!" I snorted, trying to breathe in the refreshing aroma of my barf-embellished vest. "Move it, creeps. This had better be over soon."

We skirted a particularly ripe garbage pile. "Ahh!" I said. "That's better." We all paused, inhaling deeply.

Vanya sniffled. "I wanna go home."

Georgina unfurled a wing, shading Vanya from the harsh glare. The young witch pointed. Nearby a hunched brown creature poked at the heap. His wrinkled fingers waved the trash fumes up into his face. With raspy breaths, he sucked up the smells.

"He doesn't have much time left," said Zelda. "Most here don't. Too much fresh air takes its toll. Homesickness. Sunshine. And those bloodthirsty Minotaurs."

"Ummm, those Minotaurs," said Oliver, twisting a strip in his hand. "They didn't really mean it, about eating those monsters trying to escape."

"Don't stay long enough to find out." Zelda cackled, but it sounded more like a sob than a laugh. "There's no end of ways Exxillium can do a misfit in."

Misfits couldn't appreciate true monstering, like me. I grunted and raised my snout into the air. Still, I was glad the too-fresh air didn't hold any scent of well-done exiles.

"Why don't you just fly away?" asked Georgina.

Zelda slammed down the shovel. A wart stood at attention on her green nose. Her wrinkles stretched nearly smooth on her forehead. "I can't fly. That's why I'm here. I'm a witch who's afraid of heights. Afraid of flying."

A soft "oh" fell from Georgina's lips. She extended her other wing toward the witch. Zelda pushed her face into Georgina's. "Do you think you have all the answers? Or are you just feeling sorry for me? I'm telling you, they'd cut your wings back if they sent you here for good. You wouldn't be able to fly either. No more soaring or dipping or loopty-loops. You wouldn't be able to get away—even if you tried."

Zelda's eyes stormed. She clamped shut her mouth and pulled her hat even lower over her face. Without another word, she led the way up a short hill to level ground.

Pretending I swung a broadaxe in one hand, I pushed

FROM the GRAVE

Georgina and Vanya back into line and kicked Frank in the knee for good measure. Oliver already stumbled close behind Zelda. I wondered if the witch had attempted to escape yet. Nah, she'd have been a barbecue bone sandwich for the Minotaurs if she'd tried and failed. Maybe that's why she was so bitter. She knew escape was impossible and her time here was short. My tail twitched. She'd been born a freak, hadn't she? Either fix it or forget it. Monster or die!

Although I guess it was a good thing I wasn't a witch, since it turns out I was afraid of heights too. I yanked on my hair tuft. Snotfargle! Too much thinking and not enough monstering! I was a troll! A McNastee troll. It didn't matter to a troll about heights, and no true-blood McNastees would ever end up on Exxillium!

Zelda stopped at a freshly tilled plot of ground. She pointed with the shovel handle, making an invisible arc across the field. "Here we are."

"This the cemetery?" asked Oliver. "I don't see any tombstones and coffins."

Zelda cackled and shook her head. "Well, I guess we do bury stuff here. But not bodies. No cemeteries in Exxillium. Haven't you been listening to me? Monsters here either implode or fizzle up from the sun. Nothing really left to bury." She held out a handful of black seeds. "This is our garden, and I'm on the planting crew." Plunging her shovel into the ground, she dug a hole and dropped in the seeds with a handful of bat poop. Quickly she filled the hole with sandy soil, tamping it down with the blunt side of the shovel. A crooked smile crept across her face. "Want to join in the fun, anyone?" She cackled crazily, nearly bending in two before finally recovering and shuffling on to begin another hole.

"You're looney too," I said, shielding my face with my claw. "And I'm already fizzling up. I'm getting out of this sunshine!"

Zelda paid me no attention. She dug at a more frantic pace. Her words sped up as well.

"We have to grow some of our food. The rest we harvest from the trees, different round gourds and mushy stuff. Sticky and sweet."

I grimaced. My senses overloaded. My feet not moving like I wanted them to do.

"Or if we're lucky, a dead fish will wash ashore."

"No Gurglenut Chewies?" asked Oliver, peering through his slits.

"Or sludge noodles?" said Vanya.

"Or crud crumb pie?" said Georgina.

"Or fester juice?" Frank croaked.

My own dry throat watered at the thought.

Zelda shook her head. "We collect rainwater and flavor it with moldy fruit and fermented seaweed." She jabbed the shovel into the dirt, then pushed back a strand of flyaway hair. She stared into the distance. "I've been told that once in a while we get to feast on grub, worms, or maggots. And maybe dance the monster mash on the beach around a small fire. Until the Minotaurs break it up anyway."

"Like a Mid-Winter Festival bonfire?" said Vanya.

With a flick of her gloved fingers, Zelda tossed more seeds and bat poop into the hole. "Nothing here is like back in Uggarland," she said. "Nothing! This is the end of the world as you'll ever know it. Understand?"

Vanya collapsed on the ground, sobbing like a mourning specter. Georgina hiccupped a gurgle. Dragon drool leaked from her lips. Frank stood wringing his big blue hands, and Oliver trembled in his wrappings.

I shifted from hoof to hoof. It was even more awful here than I imagined. No wonder misfits sometimes attempted an escape—even knowing what the Minotaurs would do when they caught them. Death sounded a heap better than this dump.

Zelda continued scooping dirt over the hole and *bam! bam! bam!* pounding it flat, like she was burying a body.

I grabbed the shovel from her hands. "Enough already. They get the picture."

"But do you?"

The teen witch locked me in a stare. Her green hands slid over my orange claws. An energy seemed to flow from her to me. I swear my head expanded bigger than an inflated bully ball. Pictured scenes from my life trailed in twisting lines through my brain.

Zap! Suddenly the scenes stopped spinning by. One brightly colored scene fixed in place. Nelly. In our apartment courtyard. Yesterday. With the mutant beast.

"Kit-ty," she said, stroking the mutant white, fluffy fur. "Pret-ty kitty."

"Give it here, Nelly!" I grabbed a clawful of fur. I jammed the ugly thing into my baggy pants' pocket and raced away into the Phantom Street gloom.

Zap! The scene was gone. My head shrunk to normal size. Zelda pulled back her hands and looked away.

I snorted and threw down the shovel. "Get away from me, witch!"

"Malcolm, you okay?" the dragon asked. The other three misfits stood there staring at me like I'd broken out in purple polka-dots.

I grunted. "Just need some foul air. And no witches! Finish up the tour. I'll meet you goons later."

Frank's eyes studied me as I stepped away. He'd hung out with plenty of witches. Maybe he even knew about this tricky mind-messing spell the teen witch had pulled on me.

"Hey," Vanya called after me in a voice filled with panic. "You're not leaving the island now, are you?"

Before I could take another step, Frank's surprising words stopped me.

"The witches won't go without us, Malcolm."

I whirled around, facing the five misfits. He stood in the middle of them. Somehow he seemed taller than the dragon and more gruesome green than the witch. I stomped my hoof. He was right. The witches would refuse to abandon even one of these infuriating misfits.

This time Frank had out-monstered me without a single punch. With a snort, I turned back down the hill, quickly making my way to the smoky trash heap. Collapsing in a dark corner behind a palm tree, I dropped my tufted head onto my bent knees and groaned. I couldn't take much more of this torment—not even for Principal Snaggle.

Then to top it all off, that crazy Gooney plopped down next to me.

"Our trash heap's not up to Monster City standards, of course," said Gooney. "But decay wasn't built in a day, right?" He giggled.

"I guess so," I muttered, breathing deep. Ahhh! That was a little better. A smoky bouquet, tinged with a hint of mild mold and a handful of rotted fish entrails—if I wasn't mistaken.

While I tried to regain my monster mojo, the zombie chit-chattered away. The mutant's noise grated on my pointy ears, worse even than Mr. Wartwood's math lessons. But the garbage aroma was too invigorating to leave.

"You look so familiar to me." Gooney tapped his droopy forehead, squishing three wrinkles into one large one. "Like somebody famous."

I shrugged.

"Well," said Gooney with a goofy smile, "maybe a few jokes will get you talking." He rambled on and on and on, one awful joke after the other. By the time he asked me, "Why was the skeleton so lonely?" I was on the verge of implosion.

"Stop with the jokes!" I didn't want to know about a stupid lonely skeleton. Maybe if I started yakking this crazy goon would shut up. I took a deep decay-scented breath then launched into a long family history. "My grandma Ooogle was the famous one, okay? She was the head of B.A.D.—before she was killed in an accident. I look a lot like her. My dad, Roary, was famous too. The Monster City Scandals had a front page picture of him when he was killed in a Scare Patrol mission years ago."

Gooney squinted and sucked in his lopsided lower lip. "That wouldn't be Roary McNastee now would it? Awful business with that fire he got into."

"Yeah."

For a few heartbeats, Gooney stayed silent—but not for long. His mouth took off again. "Ready for one more joke?"

"No! Just shut your trap."

Gooney giggled but before he could say anymore, I continued the sad and glorious McNastee story.

Halfway through, after talking about the fire that killed my dad, Gooney chimed in. "Nothing most monsters fear more than an out-of-control fire." He giggled again. "But we do love playing with fire, don't we? Ever the temptation to control what destroys us. Such monsters!"

Although I'd warned him not to, I could tell he was about to start another joke, so I kept on talking, jabbering about anything I could think of. Funny thing was that once I started spilling my guts (so to speak), I didn't want to stop. It was sort of a relief to talk to someone—even Gooney.

"My mom's a true-blood troll. She works hard to support

the three of us, sewing Halloween costumes at the Ghouls 'R Us store. She makes just enough to bring home the sludge noodles and, well, pay for a place for us. Not exactly a home but . . ."

"A less-than-desirable roof over your heads and tails," cut in Gooney with a chuckle.

I elbowed him. "Hey, don't interrupt me."

He nodded and swallowed another giggle.

"So like I was saying, I have a little sister. Nelly. She's three-and-a-half." I took a deep breath of smoky air. "She ah, calls me 'Mo-Mo.' And I help my mom out, you know."

I stopped short because when I'd started talking about my mom and Nelly, I guess some smoke from the trash heap blew into my eyes. I wiped a claw across them. "I'm teaching Nelly to be monster strong. Like my dad. And my grandma."

My mouth seemed as out of control now as Aldolfo's bus. "But I worry about her, you know. What if Nelly isn't monster strong? Last summer when I played video games at my friend Ghoulbert's, I took her along. She always ended up with Frank. She'd help him fold his clothes or tidy his already neat freak room. Once I found him showing her how to wash laundry with soapy water and a scrub brush. I never took her back again."

Gooney cleared his throat. "I've heard worse."

I cast my eyes about me. "Yeah, here in Exxillium I bet you've seen and heard much worse. Too much light. Too much fresh air. Too little dirt and dread and drear. Too awful!"

I yanked on my hair tuft, welcoming the pain. "There's no way Nelly is ever gonna end up here. Never! Not if I can help it."

I jammed my fisted claw against my chest and made a solemn true-blood troll promise. I'd leave no gravestone standing to keep my Nelly out of Exxillium!

CHAPTER EIGHT

Monster Rule #99: Never talk to strangers, except when you are the stranger.

FRANK'S TALE

Zelda brushed off her gloves as she watched Malcolm walk away. "Guess he wasn't enjoying the tour."

"Or our company," said Georgina.

The teen witch nodded and motioned for us to follow. "I almost forgot the most important thing the guards told me to show you." She cackled, sounding crazy again—like pre-implosion crazy. Taking an overgrown trail through the center of the island, she directed us past thick green ferns and dense bushes. The lesser-used route was a shorter, direct path back to the communal hut. We skirted the opposite side of the dump before arriving at the camp area.

"Here we are," Zelda said, stopping by a large, swaying tree at the back of the community hut. A plaque was nailed there. The strange tree's bright green, frothy leaves bent back and forth, back and forth. I grabbed the trunk to steady myself. More Exxillium sensory overload.

Zelda pointed at the sign. "There it is. The official new law

President Vladimir enacted, in case you haven't heard. Listen up because those Minotaur creeps said I had to warn you."

"What do you mean?" Georgina asked. "Warn us about what?"

"Outlawed stuff," said Vanya pointing at the sign. Even with only one eye, Vanya was the fastest reader in our O.M.O. classroom.

"Officially outlawed." Zelda tapped the sign with a pointy fingernail. She began to read aloud.

HEAR YE, HEAR YE,

By the order of PRESIDENT FOULTON VLADIMIR the THIRD, pursuant to his powers enumerated in Article 1, Section II, forthwith amends the Monster Constitution of Uggarland. Amendment 1. Section I. A monster who displays any unusual colorations or actions—deemed as such by the local authority figure as detailed below—will be under surveillance by the appointed authorities until (a.) said monster can alter his/her appearance and (b.) conduct him/herself in a manner approved by the monster community.

Amendment 1. Section II. If the above-mentioned monster continues to exhibit behavior abhorrent or inappropriate to the monster community, said monster will be transported to Exxillium and remain there permanently.

Amendment 1. Section III. Sentencing of errant monsters will be determined by (a.) the local magistrate for adult monsters and (b.) the school principal for student monsters, ages ten to fifteen. In cases where the wayward monster attempts to elude authorities or causes major disruption to the monster community requiring immediate action, the monster shall be EXECUTED.

Dated: Shocktober 1, Year of the Scrull

Effective immediately.

"That means us," gasped Oliver.

"This can't be right," said Georgina shaking her head. "They don't send kids to Exxillium."

"Or execute them," I whispered.

Zelda's green face twisted into a crazed mask—slitted eyes pulled down, cracked lips pulled up. "Until now," she said. "Isn't it funny. Not until now. Lucky us!" She tossed her black-hatted head from side to side, cackling uncontrollably.

Oliver, Vanya, Georgina, and me stood in front of the edict, mouths hanging open. At only eleven, I wasn't ready to consider my coffin design.

After I'm not sure how long, Zelda finally stopped her wild laughter.

Her voice shook slightly when she spoke. "I was the first fourteen-year-old to be sent here. Shocktober 2nd. Just one day after the president's new law was enacted. Ha! I'll probably be listed in the monster history books!"

My stomach felt as though I still flew loopty-loops on Witch Picklepuss's broom. President Vladimir meant business. It seemed as though all the misfit wiggle room had been removed—even for young misfits like us. A quivering Oliver tugged on a loose wrapping, unwinding it farther. Georgina's wings fluttered, stirring up more fresh air. Vanya pressed a perfumed handkerchief to her tear-filled eye.

"Hey," said Zelda, scanning our faces, "don't you four dare implode on me. You still have a chance to stay out of this place. So . . . so monster up!"

"But my granny told me I was already monster enough," I murmured, not meaning to say the words out loud. Granny and The Rules didn't agree on me. I couldn't wrap my head around it all. Which should I believe?

"You're monster enough—for a dead monster." Zelda pressed

a hollowed-out gourd into my hands, but the effort of taking a drink seemed overwhelming right now.

"That brings us to the end of our tour." Zelda swept her hat off and bowed.

The DEAD end, she meant.

"You've only got a little time left," she said. "So enjoy your day in paradise!" Zelda's crazed cackle followed us four as we shuffled away like zombies on parade. Georgina and Vanya crowded under a small tree. Oliver headed for a semi-dark corner of the community hut. "Let's wait in here," he said with a shaky voice. I started to follow when a troll, with skin so dark he seemed more brown than orange, waved his claw at me. He motioned me to join him beneath a shady palm tree at the dump's inner edge.

My hand, too, sent a painful signal. I rubbed at my burning palm, sensing somehow a pull toward the troll. Granny's magic or Exxillium's insanity?

"I'll be right back," I said to Oliver.

As I drew closer, I could see even more monsters ringing the trash heap, sucking in the smells. Far on the other side, I spied Malcolm. He was turned away from me, bent low, and leaning toward an exiled monster. I narrowed my eyes against the sun's glare. Malcolm seemed to be jabbering to the silly zombie who'd greeted us earlier on the beach. Was Exxillium messing with Malcolm too—forcing him to hang out with misfits?

The troll motioned to me again. Something about his face seemed vaguely familiar. But it was difficult to make out the monster's features as he sat half-hidden in the shadows. I didn't know anyone on Exxillium. Did I?

"Over here. Hurry." The troll's raspy voice rose from the dim. "Over here, Frank." The last word, an intense whisper, sliced through my brain fog.

"Who . . . who are you? And how do you know me?" I dropped to the sand. I'd heard that voice before.

The troll motioned me still closer. He leaned his wrinkled, bumpy face toward mine. "I recognized you by your blue skin."

I winced and drew back.

The troll shook his head. "No. I didn't mean any offense. You stand out in a crowd of monsters, is all I meant. And of course, I recognized your Frankenstein shoulders. Just like your father's."

"Who are you?" Each of my words held a hint of anger mixed with fear.

The troll tilted his face. I couldn't tell if he grinned or grimaced. "Don't you recognize me? But maybe . . . maybe you were too young."

"Too young for what? How do you know my dad? Did you work with him at the Haunted House Factory?" My fingers tightened into fists.

"No. I was a banker." The troll reached out a shaky claw, rested it on my shoulder, and sighed. I stiffened as a tremor shook the troll's lumpy body.

He drew back his claw and cradled it against his chest. It was just like Zelda had said—both the sunshine and the homesickness were eating this monster up. It didn't seem like he could take it much longer. He looked nearly ready to implode.

The troll's next words rattled out. "I'm Roary McNastee."

"M . . . Malcolm's dad?"

The troll nodded.

"But you can't be. I remember the night you died. Malcolm stayed at our house with Ghoulbert and me. We were playing Skullduggery and Count the Boogers. All kinds of fun stuff."

I stopped abruptly, looking in Malcolm's direction. He still faced away from us on the other side of the trash heap. I sucked in a smoky breath, remembering. Before his dad's death, we'd often play together. Games like Hide-n-Scare with Ghoulbert. All of us would climb high and higher up the cemetery skeleton trees. We'd howl at the half moons and brag about what monsters we'd be.

Back then, he hadn't cared that I was an odd monster out. And after his dad was gone, Malcolm—well, he became Malcolm.

"As you can see," said the troll, "I didn't die that night."

"But I remember. I was only six or seven. We . . . we took Malcolm back home the next morning. And a Bigfoot was there."

The troll broke in. "That was Doubledose Tankster, I'm sure. My best friend. We were on the Scare Patrol together."

"But Doubledose came back and you—I mean—Malcolm's dad didn't. Doubledose was the only monster that returned to Uggarland that night." I paused, looking away—finding it too difficult to stare a dead person in the face. My words tumbled out. "Doubledose said he warned you not to go into the house. But you didn't listen. That you wanted to scare the humans to death. Monster or die—just like the Scare Patrol Code. And right after you went in, there was a big explosion. Windows busted. Fire shot out. No monsters got out alive.

"I remember Malcolm practically tackling Doubledose and pulling on his shaggy beard then. He yelled, 'Why didn't you save him? Why didn't you save my dad?' And Doubledose picked him up and held him tight saying he couldn't—not with all that fire."

I gulped, trying to catch a glimpse of Malcolm through the trash heap smoke. He'd been so angry, so violent that day confronting Doubledose—and he'd never really stopped, had he? Maybe Malcolm was still that scared little monster who'd lost his dad.

The troll's cracked lips pulled up. "Sounds like Doubledose told a good tale all right. I made him promise to tell everyone I'd died in the fire. So my family wouldn't have to bear the stigma of my exile here. You see, I learned that the magistrate had found out about me. That I would be exiled soon. I turned myself in on the sly." He paused, rubbing a wrinkled claw across his face. "Money can buy silence. The right amount of money paid to the right monsters."

My neck bolts buzzed. There, hanging from the troll's neck, was a duplicate of the lucky shark's tooth Malcolm always wore. Some luck it had brought. This really did seem to be Malcolm's dad. Still, could I trust him any more than I did Malcolm? He was a McNastee after all. "Why not just die in the fire if you knew you were being exiled?"

Malcolm's dad growled low. "That would have been the easy way out. I had hopes though. Of making it out of exile. Changing things somehow—with a little time. That's what's kept me hanging on here."

"Why were you exiled?" I asked. "What did you do? Did you steal money from the bank?"

"If only that's all I'd done," he said with a hoarse chuckle.

I could understand a power hungry monster doing that. He might even be applauded for an act like that—on the sly, of course, as long as he didn't take the money from a too important monster. Or the monster didn't find out.

Roary McNastee smiled a sad smile. "I got caught helping humans escape from the Scare Patrols."

"What!" The word exploded from my mouth. Several of the other monsters looked our way. I looked to where Malcolm had been sitting. But he'd vanished from the other side of the trash heap. Malcolm must not have recognized his dad, for surely if he'd seen him, he'd have been here with him.

"I know monsters are supposed to hate humans," said Malcolm's dad. His words were barely louder than a whisper. "We are to hate them no matter whether they're young or old. Hate them with a passion. I thought I did. I wanted only to follow The Rules. Not question them. Not try to change them. Monster rules rule."

He paused. His gnarled claw pulled at his gray whiskers. "But one stormy night, at a typical Scare Patrol, I came face to face with a young mother. She held her boy child tight. The two of them reminded me of my own Wanda and little Malcolm. How could I destroy the humans? Even frighten them? They were frightened enough. She pleaded with me for mercy."

Roary McNastee twisted his lips into a crooked seam. "So during all the confusion, I snuck them away to what I hoped was a safe place. Hid them in a forest hollow. The boy child touched my face when I was ready to go. His little hand was the softest thing I've ever felt."

Mr. McNastee fell silent, but I had to know more. "If you did it just that one time, how did the authorities find out? About you saving humans?"

"Cause it wasn't just that one time. After that, I stopped following the Scare Patrol rules. Especially if there was a family. I tried to save dozens of humans before they caught me."

I looked away, out toward the lengthening shadows, stretching all the way down to the sandy beach. I'd overheard my parents and I knew monsters managed to get away with bending The Rules occasionally. Well, monsters other than misfits it seemed.

Mr. McNastee whispered. "I sure hope that one little boy child and his mom made it out." He paused and hung his head. "But that's as looney as trying to save them is. Look what all those monster shenanigans got me. Stuck here. Without my own son. My own wife. Forever. Why couldn't I just be cruel like all the McNastees before me?"

I tried to swallow, but my throat was bone dry. I couldn't believe it. Mr. McNastee was like me. Malcolm's dad was a misfit too.

My words wobbled out. "It's hard to be what they say you have to be. When you're not what they want you to be, I mean."

Malcolm's dad laid his claw on my shoulder. "Indeed it is, Frank. But I've found that sometimes the truth lives outside of The Rules."

We sat in silence for a short while. His own misery overwhelmed mine. It seemed to hover about him like a nagging ghost. For once, I truly wished I had enough of Granny Bubbie's magic to ease his sadness, if only for a little while. I did have enough monster intuition to know his days of surviving Exxillium would soon be ended.

Oliver called to me from outside the hut. "Hurry, Frank. Zelda said it's time to go."

"Coming." I started to push myself up, but Mr. McNastee grabbed my arm.

"Quick," he said. "Tell me about them. Malcolm and my wife. My family. Tell me about my family."

"They're doing fine, I guess." I chose my words carefully, describing my enemy to his dad. I still wanted to make a fellow misfit feel a little better. "Your wife works at Ghouls 'R Us. She makes costumes."

He nodded. "Wanda. Always so good with her hands. So creative." He paused. "But she can't make much money doing that job."

I shrugged. "I guess so. I mean, they had to move out of our neighborhood. Into one of those new apartments on Phantom Street."

"Ahhhh," groaned Mr. McNastee. "But how is my boy? How is Malcolm?"

"Mean and tough and . . ." I paused, searching for the right words. "A real monster."

McNastee nodded. A slow smile pulled at the corners of his lips.

A closer howl, from one of the Minotaurs I was sure, echoed into our shadowed shelter. "Monster round-up! Now!"

Oliver waved some loose strips above his head. "Hurry, Frank!"

"I gotta go." I tried to stand, but my totally scuffed-up boots seemed rooted in the sand. It was Mr. McNastee's loneliness that held them fast. I wanted to give him one more tidbit to hold him over, until his impending implosion.

"Nelly's really a great kid too. You can be proud of her as well." I pushed myself up then.

"What?" His strong claw yanked me back. "Nelly? Who's Nelly? What do you mean?"

"Your daughter." His sharp nails dug into my wrist. "She was born about six months after you . . ."

Roary McNastee's eyes widened. His jaw hung slack.

"You didn't know, did you?" I stammered.

Roary McNastee slowly shook his head.

Oliver's voice cut into the silence. "Frank, come on! The Minotaurs are starting to swing their axes."

Roary McNastee's claw released my hand. His gruff whisper floated up on the salty sea breeze. "Will you tell them, Frank? Promise you'll tell them I love them."

With my mind a whirl of monster is and monster isn't, I stumbled away—not sure that I could keep a promise this big.

CHAPTER NINE

Monster Rule #17: Honor your family, unless it's to your advantage not to.

FRANK'S TALE

At school's end, late that afternoon after our return from Exxillium, I followed Ghoulbert out of Fiendful Fiends Academy. He was a half-head taller than me with ample padding and classic green monster skin. Ghoulbert lived for mayhem and his pet tarantula, Spidey.

"Come on you, creep!" he yelled at me. "Mam and Pap are gonna be so mad when they find out about you. The more mad they get at you, the more mad they'll probably get at me too." He shoved me forward. I tripped and bit my lip but righted myself in time. From the corner of my eye, I saw Malcolm rush into the boys' outhouse. We could hear his gagging and worse.

"Hey! Hold up, Frank. Let's go check out McNastee in the potty pit!" My big brother dragged me after him. I tried to pull away. "No, you don't. I'm keeping my eye on you."

Ghoulbert slammed his book bag against the wooden outhouse door. "Anything interesting coming up in there? Or going down?" Ghoulbert's hee-haw hoot echoed across the courtyard.

"Go away," Malcolm croaked.

"I want to find out about Exxillium." Ghoulbert pounded on the door, nearly splintering the rotting wood.

"Ask your booger of a brother about it."

I shook my head so hard that my neck bolts seemed to loosen. No way did I want to rile Malcolm right now. My head was still spinning—not from the ride back—but with all the secrets I now knew. Secrets that could destroy Malcolm. Secrets I'd sort of promised to share.

Ghoulbert spat in my direction. "I wanna hear it from you, Malcolm. I don't talk to my misfit brother any more than I have to."

Malcolm stayed silent. So did I.

Ghoulbert shouted his pleas through the door. "You can come over to my house. Mam probably made Gurglenut Chewies. You can have as many as you want."

"I'm not hungry," Malcolm muttered back. His burp echoed through the rotting walls. The return flight from Exxillium must have done him in again.

"Save some for me," squealed Ghoulbert.

"Go away!" yelled Malcolm with a kick at the door. A new, splintered hole appeared with the tip of his hoof peeking out.

Ghoulbert grunted. "Last chance. I'll let you play my Rock-em-Sock-em Monsters as long as you want."

"GO AWAY!" Malcolm burped and shot off a barrage of classic curses.

"Scumtwaddle!" Ghoulbert yelled. "You're worse than a snot-nosed, screaming human. I'm not gonna let you ever play any of my games again. And you better watch out for your little sister. Nelly told me the other day that monsters should be nice."

I gulped. Did Nelly take after her exiled father? The dad she didn't even know!

Ghoulbert muttered, "That's what Frank used to say when he was little too. I thought he'd learn better. But misfits never do!"

"Shrivel up and die," Malcolm yelled back. Ghoulbert delivered a final blow to the courtyard commode before twisting my arm behind my back and pushing me forward. "Let's go."

Grimacing, I fell into step with my big brother. I could hear Malcolm puking into the splintered black outhouse hole behind us. Malcolm had always bragged how he wanted to be like his father. He'd always blabbered on and on about how much he missed him. Did he miss him enough to learn that he still lived—on Exxillium?

"Rat splat, Frank!" said Ghoulbert with a growl. He twisted my arm still higher. "Now you've got my best friend mad at me too!"

"Sorry," I muttered, ready to duck more blows.

"He's the bestest monster at our whole school, and he's my friend. And I don't have any other friends." Ghoulbert threw a quick punch to my sore arm. I grunted. "Why're you always messing stuff up with your stupid ways?"

"I don't mean to. It's just how I am."

"Then quit being that way." He threw another punch. "Got it?"

I sucked in a deep breath of Uggarland air, wondering if I'd ever 'get it.'

BY THE TIME we neared our house in Godzilla Heights, the evening gloom was skulking in. I welcomed the familiar gray vapor. Ahhhh! So much better than Exxillium's bright blueness of sea and sky. Still, I couldn't forget the horrors there, particularly Mr. McNastee. And what his exile meant to all his family.

I dared to ask Ghoulbert a question. "Do you think Malcolm likes the place they moved to?"

Ghoulbert snorted and spat onto the uneven walkway. "What's it to you?"

"Just curious. That's all. I've never been to one of those apartments before."

"Malcolm would never let you see it. Only me, 'cause I'm his friend." Ghoulbert patted his chest and nodded. "He don't like it. Everything's still shiny and new. No cobwebs or spiders or ghosts. And they had to buy furniture from the Bad Choice Store."

I grimaced. Most of the stuff there came from the storm scavengers. They were barely civilized monsters, who lived on the edge of Uggarland, where most monsters never ventured. The scavengers hunted in the Shadowlands—the divide between the land of the humans and monsters.

A brutally evil storm from Moratorium—a Terrornado or a Horrorcane—could sometimes sweep through the Shadowlands. Whole houses might plunk down, complete with furniture and oddities. The scavengers would haul the debris to The Bad Choice Store—the only choice for those monsters who couldn't afford pricier, more appropriate monster décor.

Ghoulbert zigzagged his hand in the air. "Yeah, they've got bizarre stuff like a fringed floor lamp and this awful pink-flowered sofa." Ghoulbert spat again. "Don't tell Malcolm I told you, but he's got a purple-polka-dotted beanbag chair in his room and Nelly has one that looks like a stuffed teddy bear."

"Wow. That's bad." I twisted a neckbolt.

She ought to have a clunky skeleton chair or a cobwebbed toadstool bench. I'd heard that Uggarland spiders shied away from human furniture like that, even with a witch's warty spell.

Using both his big green hands, Ghoulbert drew a circle. "You wouldn't believe it, but there was the ugliest clock ever at Malcolm's house. It had mouse-shaped ears and yellow-gloved hands, and it squeaked the time." Ghoulbert snorted. "Rat splat! One time Malcolm threw a pillow at it, and the blasted thing jammed. That mouse kept squeaking and squeaking. Drove me so batty, I tore it from the wall and smashed it against the floor. Malcolm thanked me big time for that."

Patting his barrel-shaped chest again, Ghoulbert smiled. "That's what friends are for." Then he punched my arm, hard. "If you haven't ruined it for me."

I stumbled through the front door, clutching my arm and wondering if I wasn't going to totally ruin things for myself as well.

TRYING TO AVOID my parents for as long as possible, I ran to my room and barricaded the door. As I waited for supper though, I saw a strange sight out my bedroom window. Along the skyline, an intense orange beam of light squeezed between the gloom above and the gloom below. The determined drear was suddenly ablaze.

"No way," I muttered. It looked like the skyline approaching Exxillium. I blinked.

It was gone.

Only gray and more gray melting into blackness. Just as it should be. I rubbed my itchy right hand against my crumpled pants. Was some of Granny Bubbie's magic messing with me? Or had the bright lights of my Exxillium excursion triggered the mirage? A leftover ray of sunshine. Or perhaps a niggling reminder of Zelda and Mr. McNastee and all the other odd monsters out, trapped beneath the glare.

Zelda, not much older than me, but already banished. Doomed to a short, awful life, waiting to implode.

Mr. McNastee, a father without a family, never to meet Nelly. He'd never know how much his daughter liked wearing different

Central Islip Public Library

costume parts that her mom brought home from work. He'd never hug his wife again or eat her homemade sludge noodles or admire all the hand-stitched costumes she designed. He'd never help Malcolm lead a Junior Scare Patrol mission or hear him practice his growl or see his horns fully grown out.

Mr. McNastee had asked me to tell them how much he still loved them and missed them. But how could I face telling my nemesis Malcolm? I held my head in my hands and groaned.

Still, didn't Nelly deserve a chance to have a dad? My pap and I might not see eye to eye all the time, but I believed he wanted the best for me. That he'd always be there for me. We were family.

Surely Mr. McNastee was more than monster enough for his family. Maybe they could even get his name cleared. They were McNastees after all. What if they could free him from Exxillium? Malcolm might not hate me anymore, and he'd be Ghoulbert's friend like before.

All the while I debated Mr. McNastee's exile, my right hand burned. I rubbed it against my chest. The heat from it seemed to fire up my heartbeat.

"Should I tell or not, Granny?" I whispered the words. But only the sound of our house ghosts swooshing about in the attic above answered back. The ghosts shrieked and moaned periodically for good measure. Every respectable monster home had at least three. Well, except for Malcolm's.

I stuck my head out into the hallway. No Ghoulbert or Mam or Pap around. A spicy whiff of peppered innards tickled my nose. I licked my lips. Ghoulbert was most likely in the kitchen drooling over the pot—and Pap as well—while Mam tried to shoo them away. I had perhaps a few minutes only before being summoned.

Shuffling my Frankenstein feet as quietly as possible over the appropriately creaky floorboards, I picked up the cobwebbed phone. The heat in my hand cooled. Was that a good or bad sign? I trembled as I imagined Malcolm on the other end of the line reaching for his family's mouse-shaped telephone. I took a deep breath and dialed.

"For Nelly," I said. "And Mr. McNastee . . . and Malcolm too."

CHAPTER TEN

Monster Rule #19: When the truth compromises monstering,
it's best to lie.

MALCOLM'S TALE

Slithering shrouds of the evening's gray mist twisted around my legs. I'd finally recovered enough to pull myself from the outhouse and stumble down Phantom Street. My hot, dry skin drank in the dampness. I breathed a tired sigh and pushed my hooves against the uneven walkway, forcing myself to hurry. I didn't want to arrive home late, or Mom would ask questions. Questions I didn't want to answer, even though I wasn't sure why.

"Ugggh! Less thinking and more monstering," I muttered.

I pulled myself up the steep apartment steps, jiggled the too-shiny brass doorknob, and slammed the door behind me. An eyeful of the awful pink-flowered sofa nearly caused me to gag again.

"Snotfargle!" I smeared a dirty claw across the floral nightmare. "Cast off junk."

I know my mom was lucky to have found a job at the Ghouls 'R Us store. Year-round, she sewed special costumes for the annual Halloween Feast. Many monsters, both young and old, liked dressing up as different scary creatures or even grotesque humans. My mom could make most anything. Still, she earned next to nothing.

Just looking at the fringed floor lamp behind the couch brought on a new string of curses from me.

"Tangled twits! Dragon doo-doo! Bunion pus!"

I punched a cushy cushion and flopped onto the couch. My stomach still rumbled. I needed to be rid of this day. I didn't dare think about the ride back from Exxillium. All the twists and turns, hanging upside down while plunging through the black clouds at breakneck speed.

"Urrrp!" I rubbed my stomach. I vowed never, ever, never to visit Exxillium again, or to ride a witch's broom, or to associate with witches and mutants. Trolls were given hooves for a reason—we belonged on the ground. Monster ground. Uggarland.

I sank back onto the couch. My mom and Nelly would be here soon. That thought should have brought me some comfort, but instead—probably because of the teen witch's mind-messing magic—I remembered yesterday's horror with my little sister.

Last Scareday, Nelly had scared me half to death. I was sneaking up on a white fuzzball in our apartment courtyard. I could have fun teasing the mutant cat—playing Monster Mash or Bouncy, Bouncy Beast. But I'd forgotten Nelly was nearby.

Her bristly purple hair-sprout flopped over her pudgy orange face as she jumped up and down. Her short legs skipped across the courtyard. I reached her side too late. She already held the kitten in her arms.

"No," I started to say, ready to rip the mewing critter out of her messy troll claws. But when Nelly looked up to me with soft yellow eyes, I froze in place.

"Kit-ty," said Nelly, stroking the soft fur. "Pret-ty kitty."

I shook my head. No, this wasn't a pretty kitty. It was an awful ugly kitty. A pure white kitty with a pink nose and pale blue eyes like that freak Frank had. Monsters liked black cats. Blue-black hissing cats, arching up with flashing green eyes. Not a gross soft white kitty like this. Why couldn't Nelly see this white freak was hardly good enough for harpy food?

"Give it here, Nelly!" I said, grabbing it and stuffing it into my pocket. I had to get rid of this before Ghoulbert or another monster saw Nelly petting it. What if Principal Snaggle saw Nelly with the freaky white cat and thought she was an odd monster out?

Nelly didn't scream or yell or stamp her hoofed feet like a normal monster three-year-old would. Instead she held out her little hands and whispered, "Oh, Mo-Mo. Let me hold it. Just one time." Without even a trace of magic in her true-blood troll veins, my little sister bewitched me. My hand scrunched around the kitty's fragile neck relaxed. I eased it from my pocket and handed it back to Nelly.

"Okay," I heard myself whisper in a voice as soft and fuzzy as the kitty.

Nelly cradled the cat in orange arms. She rubbed her cheek against its white fur. "So soft." She looked up to me and smiled.

I snorted. What was wrong with me? I'd almost smiled back then. What sort of a monster example was I setting for her? I was as bad as Frank. As any of the mutant monsters. I was teaching Nelly to be less than a true-blood troll.

I had bitten down hard on my lip then and licked away a spurt of blood. The sharp tang stirred up my monster sensibilities. I stomped my hoof.

"Monster is as monster does, Nelly. No monster should like to pet fluffy, white kitties. No good. No good." I shook my head and pointed to the kitty. Nelly had to learn right from wrong, that was all.

I ripped the kitten out of Nelly's hands. Still, I had to shut my ears to her cries as I raced out of the yard.

FROM the GRAVE

I ran down the street, past Fiendful Fiends Academy, past the Haunted House Factory and Monster City Cemetery Park. When I glanced behind me, I swore I caught a glimpse of blue behind a skeleton tree. The kitty meowed in my pocket. No way could I be caught with this thing. I kept running. I ran straight to the smoking city dump. Without taking a breath, I held the white kitten high—ready to drop it on top of a smoldering heap.

"Meow." The kitty's pale blue eyes pleaded for mercy.

I don't know why, but I hesitated. Even though inside my head I could hear my monster self yelling, *Drop it! Toss it down! Leave it! NOW!*

I was like a sleepwalking zombie. My head rolled from side to side. My lower lip quivered. In slow motion, I drew the kitten to my chest. My arm seemed to have a mind of its own. I tucked the creature inside my vest.

With glances to the left and right, I slunk down the second alley from the dump gateway. I counted the dark houses which all seemed so alike on that street. Then I pulled to a stop and crouched behind a thorny jangleberry bush. Aldolfo's house. I was almost sure this was it. What a prank this would be on the misfit. Perhaps he'd be discovered hiding a mutant cat—especially if I reported on him.

No one in sight. I sprinted to the back door, careful to avoid the rotten floorboards. Ready to drop the soft kitten into the cobwebbed trashcan. I pulled a piece of crumpled paper out. With a marker I used for graffiti, I scribbled, "Kitty in can."

I remember my breath caught in my throat then. The kitten's faint thrumming purr vibrated against my chest. I froze. It was so like Nelly's heart thump-bumping against mine when I held her pressed close for a monster hug. Snotfargle! Did I hope, for Nelly's sake, that Aldolfo would keep the cat? That a freak monster would welcome a freak pet?

"Goober guts!" *Less thinking and more monstering!*

Cynthia Reeg

I dropped the cat into the can and pounded my fist on the door. With my powerful hooves, I vaulted over the porch railing and ran down the deserted alley. I didn't look back to see if the knock had been answered—or if anyone had seen my escape.

But my monster instincts sensed that Frank had seen at least some of it. All the more reason to end his time in Uggarland permanently.

Feet shuffled now, outside the apartment door. It popped open and Nelly trotted through.

"Mo-Mo! Mo-Mo! We're home!"

She raced across the small room and jumped ker-blam into my lap.

"Ooof!" Nelly's hooves jammed into my already unsettled stomach.

"Look." Nelly thrust one arm close to my face. She sported a feathery costume sleeve. "I'm a harpy. Look. I can fly." With arms flapping, she leaped off me and circled the sofa. Nelly loved going to work with Mom.

I tried to hold up my claw in a shaky monster salute, but I couldn't keep my eyes on her dizzy circles and flapping. Instead, I closed them and leaned back into the ugly pink couch.

"Here," said Nelly, sliding to a stop. She pried my eyes open and shoved a cowboy hat on my head. "Play with me."

"You know I don't wear costumes." I yanked the hat off. "Trolls are monster enough." I made a scowl so hideous that it brought a shriek from Nelly. She took off flapping again.

"Go on, Nelly," I said. "We'll play later."

"Promise, Mo-Mo?"

"Yeah, yeah. I promise."

My mom's cold claw touched my forehead. "Are you not feeling well?" She clutched a sack of sludge noodles against her chest.

I grunted. "Just tired." I shrugged her off. Even as I tried to

106

stand, the overpowering aroma of freshly sliced sludge noodles threatened to push me back down. "I'm not, burp, hungry either."

I shoved past her and a flapping Nelly, slammed my bedroom door, and collapsed on my rumpled moss blanket. Its scent of forest gloom eased me some. A fairly flat, stuffed vulture hung over my bed. I'd found the road kill last year and tried to mount it like Principal Snaggle had with his deceased pet vulture, Vincent. But my vulture, with its droopy wings extended and half its feathers missing, wasn't nearly so well preserved. Nope, but it was triumphant. Mine seemed risen from the grave. It was no thrift store trash.

Laying beneath my vulture's welcoming glare, I still felt as though I soared through the sky. My head whirled. I squeezed it with both claws, trying to banish the dizziness.

But an unsettling picture spun inside my head. That of a strangely familiar troll on Exxillium. The one whose muffled voice had almost carried into the bushes where I'd hidden, spying on Frank. The Minotaurs had called for our departure before I'd had a chance to draw close enough. I tugged on the shark tooth pendant at my neck. A strangely familiar troll.

With a grunt, I stumbled from the bed to the open window. Leaning out, I inhaled a deep breath of swampy air. There. That was a much better.

"Huh?" I opened my eyes wide, peering toward the horizon. An intense reddish, golden glow cracked the divide between land and sky. My heart skipped a beat. I blinked. It was gone. Only gloom, as always. Had a sliver of Exxillium somehow lit up the skyline? Was the young witch's magic calling to me across the waves?

"Snotfargle!" Too much thinking and not enough monstering. I knew what I needed to do. I lurched up from the bed and quietly opened the door. Nelly's high-pitched voice carried from the kitchen. My mom and sister must still be making dinner. I slipped into the hallway on silent hooves. The door to my mom's bedroom stood slightly ajar. I eased it open without a sound and crept inside. I switched on the battery-powered candle on her nightstand, another hideous Bad Choice Store buy. There next to it was a photograph of my parents on their wedding day.

My breath came now in quick pants. I drew the picture up closer to my eyes. I groaned. Even in this dim light, I quickly saw the resemblance to the monster on Exxillium. The puckered snout. The slightly crooked horns. One pointed ear flopped down. I growled.

Rubbing the back of my claw against my mouth, I recalled who had taught me to growl so long ago in the same foggy cemetery hush. The half moons had hovered in the inky sky. My dad had held me in his hefty troll arms. I was a pudgy toddler then, not even as big as Nelly was now.

My dad carried me high on his shoulders, chanting monster medleys as he climbed to the leveled mound top. He plopped me down among the stickery weeds and crafted a wondrous growl.

I clapped and barked a silly imitation. My dad nodded and repeated even more slowly his grumbly growl. I attempted another, and then another, and another. And each time my dad nodded.

Now I jumped as the stupid mouse-shaped telephone on the nightstand rang. With my free claw, I grabbed it, barely able to control my shaking.

"Who's this?" I barked.

No answer.

I growled. "Hey, booger brains!" I can hear you breathing. "Don't mess with me."

"Malcolm?"

I sucked in a breath. "Make it fast and furious, freak! Or I'm hanging up right now." One of the Gordons' house ghosts shrieked bloody murder in the background.

Frank's voice was barely above a whisper. "Did you, ah, see that troll I was talking to on Exxillium?"

"Flying farts, you twit!" My legs wobbled so badly I had to lean against the wall to keep from collapsing. "I don't care which of those mutants you jabbered with. Go stuff yourself!"

"Wait, Malcolm! Don't hang up. He wasn't just any troll . . . he's your dad."

"You about to implode or something? You are beyond looney! My dad died in a Scare Patrol fire." I drew the family photo closer. My chest tightened.

"But he didn't die. He was sent to Exxillium for doing some stuff he shouldn't have. And . . . and just so you know I'm not making this up, he was wearing the exact same shark tooth pendant that you have."

I dropped my parents' picture to the floor and ripped the shark pendant from my neck, flinging it down as well. "No! You lying, misfit maggot! My dad's a hero."

Frank paused. "Doubledose lied. I thought you—and your family—should know. Your dad misses you a lot. He said he loves you."

My enemy's words came faster and faster, beating against my ear like gut punches. "Your dad had Doubledose make up the part about him dying in the fire, so you and your mom and all the others wouldn't know they were sending him to Exxillium. But I was thinking that maybe you could help bring him back, so he can meet Nelly and be with your family again . . ."

"You freaking liar!" I spat the curse into the phone. "If this is you trying to monster up by making harassing calls, you dialed the wrong number. And you know I'm gonna make you pay for it. Don't you ever talk about my dad again!"

I slammed down the phone. I couldn't hear any more. I fell back against the bed. All the dizziness had returned. He was a monster exile. Not a hero.

No! It couldn't be true. It was some fluke. My eyes and ears had played tricks on me. It was the sickness from the flying. Frank was lying. Frank was trying to hurt me. To be cruel.

My tail uncurled and hung limp. I shook my head. No. A misfit like Frank couldn't be monsterly like that, could he? He was no master of mayhem. He was no fast-thinking wily liar like me.

I stood above the framed picture of my parents that had crashed to the floor. My dad's face stared back at me. I couldn't deny it any longer. My lips quivered. "You betrayed us! You . . . left me!" I slammed my hoof through glass. "You are a misfit! You are NOT my dad!"

"Malcolm!" my mom called from the kitchen. "Did you fall?"

My hair tuft stood on end. "I, ah, dropped some books is all. I'm doing my math homework."

"Need help?" Her voice sounded closer.

"No. No. I got it, Mom."

"I'll save some noodles for you if you get hungry later."

"Thanks," I said, grinding my hoof into my dad's face, then kicking the debris beneath the bed.

The mouse phone rang again.

"Flying farts!" I yelled into it. "Stop calling! I don't want to hear your mutant mouth ever again!"

"McNastee?" Principal Snaggle's voice thundered from the receiver. "Is that you, McNastee? Quite the answering protocol, I must say. Is that something new your substitute is teaching in Monster Etiquette?"

"Sir, Principal Snaggle, sir. I . . . thought you were . . ."

"Never mind, McNastee. I've important business to discuss. Another imperative mission for you."

My tail twitched. "Another, sir?"

"Yes, indeed. With your vast experience with misfit control, I immediately thought of you for the O.M.O. bus monitor."

"Bus monitor, sir? For the misfits?"

"Excellent, McNastee! So good of you to volunteer. You are such a true-blood monster example."

My eyes flew to the shattered picture. Perhaps not so true-blood after all. "Ah . . . thank you, sir, but . . ."

"No need to thank me. You can start tomorrow. Aldolfo should have a list of all the little critters you need to pick up. Don't want to forget anyone, do we?"

"But, sir . . ."

"Make sure they stay in monster mode on the bus. Understood?"

"Sir, I . . ."

"Excellent, McNastee! I knew I could count on you."

The phone went dead before I could utter another excuse.

I snorted, pulling hard on my hair tuft. The excursion to Exxillium with four misfits had been more than enough. Misfits were taking over my life—rather than me taking over theirs. Especially Frankenstein Gordon.

I retrieved my shark tooth pendant from the floor. It seemed I needed all the luck I could get. On silent hooves, I slipped out of my mom's bedroom and back inside my dark one. I crumpled onto the messy bed, beneath my droopy vulture.

Now I knew. Knew what I had suspected for some time. Misfit blood ran through my own monster veins—and through Nelly's as well. I must make sure no one else ever found out. Or Nelly and I could be labeled misfits.

The bed truly spun then. In a whirl. Faster and faster. Could a less than true-blood troll handle the misfits tomorrow? Or would they out-monster me?

CHAPTER ELEVEN

Monster Rule #5: A monster is judged by his actions, so act up!

FRANK'S TALE

I dropped the phone back into its stylish mini-coffin container. "Twisted toe nails!" I muttered to myself. Even looney Gooney wouldn't have blabbered as much as I'd just done. I'd only meant to help the McNastees, but instead I'd screwed up again. Misfit mayhem to the max! Malcolm madder than ever. Nelly still without a dad. Mr. McNastee still a lonely exile.

With a barrel-chested moan, I joined our house ghosts' dinnertime shriekfest. Yep, things would have been much better if I'd stayed permanently on Exxillium today!

Ghoulbert's voice thundered from the dining room. "Hurry it up, bluster butt! We're all waiting on you." I stomped down the stairs. Ka-bumping out a problem with each step. What a mess I'd made of everything! But even with all that, my stomach growled. I was, after all, a Frankenstein.

I stepped into the dim shadows of our dining room. A rusty chandelier dangled above the table. Five small candles on it dripped puddles of wax onto the table below and into the food as well. I expected the subdued lighting and my parents' anxious faces, along with Ghoulbert's slobbering one. But I stopped in mid-step when I saw the centerpiece. Granny Bubbie's crystal ball. My itchy right hand prickled at the sight.

"Don't know why we're waiting on you." Ghoulbert pulled me into the empty chair beside him. "You're such a troublemaker."

My ears, as though stuffed with cobwebs, filtered out Ghoulbert's words. I reached for Granny's crystal ball. Smooth and cool. It seemed to calm any lingering heat in my right palm as my fingers held it close. I bet there were still pictures of me in there. Pictures of the two of us together. Granny Bubbie and her Frankie Prankie.

My mom moaned softly. "I got a bit sentimental this afternoon." Her voice was barely a whisper. "I just kept thinking I heard mummy's call. 'Shareeka! Shareeka!' she said to me. 'Beware. Take care. Guard your treasures, lest ye despair.'" Mam paused. For a second I thought I saw Granny Bubbie, with her floppy hat and crooked goggles, reflected in Mam's eyes.

"Ghost twattle!" sputtered Pap.

"No, I know I heard her say it. That's why I dug out her crystal ball from my chest of drawers." Mam's eyes caressed the crystal ball I clutched.

"Dingle dung!" My dad slapped both his hands down onto the table so hard I heard it crack. A few splinters drifted to the floor at my feet. He clamped a big hand around the crystal ball and snatched it from me. With only slightly more gentleness, he dropped the ball onto the table. "I thought we'd left all that witchy muddle-mush at Granny's house. No need to infiltrate our safe monster home here with risky renegade magic."

"But I wanted something to remember my mummy by." Mam flung her wispy right arm above her head in a classic phantom pose. "I miss her so!"

"We've more than enough trouble to deal with right now, Shareeka. Don't need to be inviting drama or trickery into the mix." Pap scooped a huge dollop of peppered innards onto his plate and pushed the bowl to Ghoulbert. "Eat up! All of you. Then some of us—" He froze me with his green eyes. "—have business to talk about. Unpleasant business."

Ghoulbert chortled. "Frank's in trouble. Frank's in trouble. Gonna get whacked on the double. How many smacks will it take? One, two, three . . ."

Kaboom! Pap's fist pounded the table, sending dishes skittering and the crystal ball wobbling. I heard another crack of wood. "Enough! Eat!"

Mam started to reach a misty hand out toward the crystal ball, but Pap froze her, too, with his stare. Instead, she scooted the bowl of mashed fowl feet my way. I plopped a spoonful on my plate, but I dared not look up. And so the supper went, until I reached for the last helping of bloody bloblet pudding.

"That's mine!" Ghoulbert grabbed the bowl from my hand and downed the slimy pudding with one slurp.

I'd been all set to scarf down another helping of pudding to ease some of the day's agonies. I could still smell the pudding's overripe aroma. Sour and earthy. I could almost taste its richness. Fermented blood marrow with all its tangy intensity. I groaned and clenched my once-again stinging right hand.

My brows drew together. My blood simmered. Pap's anger seemed to have fueled mine. Or, more likely, a smoldering flame had simmered in me since my return from Exxillium. I'd not let Ghoulbert think he'd bested me. "Ha! You, lard lizard! I didn't even want it. I was only going to eat it, so you couldn't have any more."

Boozle brains! I'd been to the land of exiled monsters and back. I'd seen a world of horrors he couldn't imagine. And I'd just told Malcolm of horrors he could never imagine—his father in exile. I would not be pushed around anymore. What right did the authorities have to tell me how to monster? Or to keep Mr. McNastee and Zelda trapped on that island? And I wouldn't be bullied in my own home. Like the Minotaurs, red-hot steam seemed to huff from my nostrils.

Mam's hand floated out toward mine. "No, Ffff . . . rrrrank," she moaned. But I pulled away.

Ghoulbert nudged me with his shoulder. "Don't get in bigger trouble, doofus dung." Spray from his full mouth spewed onto my face.

"Eat sugar!" I spat the words back at him and smashed the bloblet bowl over his head.

"Hey, I can give you more of that." Ghoulbert tried to crown me with the empty peppered innards bowl, but instead I tipped forward in my chair and threw a punch. The punch missed. The momentum toppled me. My Frankenstein-sized foot caught the rickety table leg on my way down.

A deafening din of broken boards, shattered dishes, and monster curses filled the air. I stared in disbelief when I saw Granny's crystal ball teeter on the crack that was once the table's center. As if in slow motion I reached for it. Blue fingers stretching, straining—knowing even as I did that I was too late. The shimmery globe crashed onto the stone floor. An explosion of colors and sounds ricocheted off the walls. A puff of something like smoke ascended to the ceiling. A translucent image of Granny Bubbie hovered there.

"Beware. Take care. Guard your treasures, lest ye despair." Granny's words vibrated against the dining room walls, repeating again and again, until growing softer and softer they faded away.

"No! No! No!" Mam shrieked. "It's gone. Gone. Gone." Her wails doused my red-hot anger.

When would I ever learn? Anger always, always led me

into trouble. This was the monster inside who terrified me. Defeated me.

Floating through my brain were images of what my anger had done over the years:

I'd smashed one of Ghoulbert's pet spiders.

I'd bruised up Oliver during a squabble.

I'd distracted Granny and caused her crash.

And now I'd obliterated a treasured memento. It was as though Granny Bubbie had died all over again. And like before, I'd been the one who'd caused her demise.

In a sad swirl, Mam rose from the floor. Her face was a pool of pain. She clutched a shimmery fragment to her chest.

A tear slipped down my cheek. Mam wiped it away.

"It wasn't your fault, Frankie."

"That's what Granny told me, too." I shook my head. I didn't believe either of them.

"Shareeka, don't call him 'Frankie'!" Pap stomped his foot. The broken table bits rattled. "He's not a baby anymore. We've got to get tough with him. No more spoiling him. No more making excuses for him." The wiry hairs on his chin mole bobbed as he spoke.

"He's still my baby," Mam said. Her voice was soft but firm. Silver-streaked strands of midnight black encircled her transparent face. She had inherited phantom genes from her father's side of the family. Granddad Zeek, with his talented vocal abilities, had been a phantom of great esteem. Now my mam's misty shape hovered, rather than rested. Her icy eyes dripped crystal tears.

Pap attempted to hug Mam, but she slipped through his bulky arms. She floated to the floor, raking her fingers through the rubble. Pap grunted. "Enough wrestling, boys." His hand seized my shirt collar and yanked me back into my righted chair. "You two can play later. Your mam and I need to talk to Frank.

Alone." Pap growled the last word at Ghoulbert, and with his eyes, pushed him from the room. Mam still moaned.

"I know this is serious," she said. "We had a call from your teacher today. I want the best for you." She squeezed my hand. The soothing coolness seeped into me and the rest of my anger disappeared.

"The best thing we can do is to make sure he acts like a monster." Pap pushed away Mam's hand and grabbed my chin. "And looks like a monster. I want all those unmonsterly clothes thrown out. Scuff up those boots. Get 'em muddy. Keep up the fighting and brawling every time it's appropriate."

"Just like tonight," I said. Sadness fueled my sarcasm.

Pap grunted. "Remember: Monster Rule #15—Evil is mayhem orchestrated for untoward purposes. Tonight's mishap wasn't evil. There was no intent for that. It was only an accident." His fingers dug harder into my chin. "But you can't run away from a little collateral damage from time to time. Be mean. Be tough. Be monsterly."

Collateral damage. Had Granny Bubbie been collateral damage? A few stitches in my heart unraveled.

Pap's fingers relaxed their too-tight grip. "We know you can do it. Gordons have always been the best of monsters. We carry the Frankenstein lineage, of course. Need I say more?" He handed me an odd-shaped tube. "Doubledose gave this to me. He said a scavenger brought this back from the Shadowlands. It's supposed to make your skin darker. Wouldn't it be something if this stuff turned your skin green like mine? Or at least brownish blue."

My eyes widened. Pap's face glowed with hope. Even his neck bolts seemed to shine brighter.

I twisted open the container. "Ooof!" A perfumey scent overwhelmed my nostrils. It reminded me of one of Vanya's forbidden perfumes. Coconuts and passion fruit. Or some other awful human combination! I shoved the potion into my pants, not even caring when the container ripped my pocket.

I'd never known how much a disappointment the color of my skin was to him. He'd be willing for me to smell this awful in order to change it. I brushed a hand through my hair. Or maybe Pap was just willing to do whatever it took to save me.

Mam spoke again. Her words dripped with layered sorrow. Each syllable a crystal tear tinkling onto the cluttered floor. "Ms. Hagmire said if you don't shape up quickly, they'll send you to Exxillium. And you'll never come back."

"It's the new president," said Pap. His words were clear and clipped. "He's gonna clean up Uggarland. If you don't watch out, you're gonna be some of the student fallout from his first round of sweeps. Monster is as monster does, Frank. You've got to monster up fast. Scare or be scared."

"We'll help you. Help you . . . help you . . . help you." Mam's mournful wail embraced me, but still my body felt as if a herd of slobapottamus had thundered across, crumpling me into a mound of disjointed blue pieces.

"It's up to you." Pap's grip on my hand tightened. "We can't do it for you. Understand?"

I opened my mouth, but said nothing.

"Do you want to be a monster?"

"Yes," I managed to whisper.

"I can't hear you?" shouted Pap.

"Yes," I mumbled back, stumbling from my chair. "Yes. Yes, I want to be a monster."

I staggered toward the stairs.

"Help me, Granny," I muttered, under my breath. "Help me show them I'm already monster enough."

IN MY TIDY room, I dropped onto my bed—too upset to smooth

out the wrinkles I was making in my moss blanket. I groaned and rolled over.

Principal Snaggle and Ms. Hagmire said to shape up. Mam and Pap said to shape up too. And the new monster law said to shape up.

But Granny had told me I was monster enough. Witch Picklepuss said I needed to believe in where I was headed. And what had Mr. McNastee said? "Sometimes the truth lives outside of The Rules."

Above me in the attic, the house ghosts wailed away. I moaned in harmony with them, blending into their chorus. House ghosts worked as a team. Their shrieks and wails doubled and tripled in intensity when they joined together.

Wait! That was it! I jumped up. Teamwork. Misfit teamwork. Witch Picklepuss had said to show the others I was monster enough, but what if we ALL showed them? Together. Would Uggarland listen to us then?

First, though, we needed time to sort out the details. If we were going to prove we were an important part of Uggarland, we couldn't do it in exile. As much as I hated the new law, it seemed the only way for now. We must conform as much as we could for the time being.

I tiptoed into the deserted hall and picked up the phone from its mini-coffin. My idea seemed so bad, as Stan and Dan would say, that maybe—just maybe—it was good. As the house ghosts howled above, I began dialing all my misfit classmates.

CHAPTER TWELVE

Monster Rule #537: Forgetting can sometimes be more clever than remembering.

MALCOLM'S TALE

While Mom read Nelly nightmare stories before bed, I slipped from the apartment sliding into the darkness like a swamp monster eases into a pool of green muck. There it was again—that vision of me slipping into icy wetness. The image was too awful to watch. Too disturbing to be real. Swimming alongside my dad, both of us gliding through murky water.

But trolls do NOT swim. Never have and never will. It was only a hallucination—somehow embedded in my brain from a long ago bedtime nightmare story.

Or was it? Could a troll with misfit blood really swim? I snorted and shook my head. All this upsetting news was totally messing with me. Less thinking and more monstering was what I needed.

I grunted and plunged into the evening darkness toward Doubledose Tankster's house, nearly erasing the disturbing vision.

In next to no time, I stood outside Doubledose Tankster's

slanting shanty near the cemetery. I tugged down my black leather vest. I needed to know what had happened to my dad. I needed to hear it from someone I could trust. Someone other than Frankenstein Gordon.

I pounded on Doubledose's door. Faint flickering light illuminated the cracks in the wood. I knew Doubledose was there. Candles were never lit and left.

No answer. I stomped my right hoof into the doorstep dirt, then kicked the door, rattling its rusty hinges.

"Boogers and bat brains! I'm coming." Doubledose's deep voice rumbled through the door. "Don't get your tails in a tangle. You're early tonight."

I grunted and stepped back as Doubledose's footsteps approached the door. A lone wolf's howl carried on the wind. I shivered. I didn't want to know if the howl was a good omen or a dire warning.

"Huh?" Doubledose stuck his hairy face through the opened doorway. His golden eyes blinked into the blackness. "Who's there?"

"Malcolm. McNastee." My voice squeaked. I snorted in disgust.

Doubledose pulled open the door. "Roary's boy?" He stepped closer. His baggy overalls hung on his skinny frame. His hard hat sat on the table, most likely discarded as soon as he had returned from his job at the Haunted House Factory. I knew he worked there with Ghoulbert's dad.

"Yeah."

Doubledose scratched his shaggy head. "Should have known. You look just like him."

I couldn't help but squirm. My tail twitched out of control. All the monster wiles I'd practiced for so long seemed to have disappeared. I snorted again.

"I haven't seen you since . . . " Doubledose paused. His paw rattled the doorknob. "Why are you here?"

"Did he really die?" The words shot out. I pushed myself into the pale pool of candlelight. "My father. In the fire."

"Isn't that what I said? Back then, so many years ago. How's a monster supposed to remember?"

"You remember. I know you do."

Doubledose still trembled but he nodded. Finally, he spoke. "I could never forget. Never forgive myself."

"Tell me."

"But it would be the ruin of me. If any other monster found out."

"I don't care." I growled low and slow, finally allowing my monster instincts to rule. But approaching footsteps forced me to pull back. I swiveled, "Huh? Who's there?"

Three monsters stomped from under the leafless skeleton trees and into Doubledose's yard.

"Hey, you adding a new a paw to our card game tonight?" I recognized Mondo Gordon's voice.

Doubledose shook his head, panting hard. "Not me. I'd never try to pull a fast one on you guys." He punctuated his words with a weak bark, trying to sound nonchalant.

"Hey, Malcolm?" Ghoulbert's dad punched my shoulder. "What are you doing here? Up to no good, I'm sure."

"As always, Mr. Gordon." I grunted and shuffled my hooves. "Just . . . ahh . . . asking about Scare Patrol. I mean, Junior Scare Patrol. It's a . . . an assignment about . . ."

"History questions," said Doubledose. "Highlights from past patrols."

"Hmmfff." Mondo Gordon shook his flat-topped head. "Ghoulbert didn't mention that. He could have interviewed me. I've been on more than my fair share of patrols."

FROM ᵗʰᵉ GRAVE

One of the other monsters, a ghostly shape almost lost in the blackness, moaned. "Parents are the last to know what's going on with their kids. Come on. Let's play Blacksplat. Not talk about little monsters. That's what I'm here to forget."

A gap-toothed gremlin pushed his way through. "I hear ya. 'Nuff nightmares at my house for any monster to handle." He shook a dusty bottle. "But I brought along something to help us forget." He elbowed Doubledose as he lumbered past. "Know what I mean?" Mondo and the other monster grunted and followed him inside.

As they passed by him, Doubledose drew his lips up to reveal a mouthful of sharp, tarnished teeth. But his monsterly grin faded fast when he looked back at me. He positioned the door between us and started to push it closed.

I jammed a hoof into the opening. "Tell me," I growled.

Doubledose shook his head. "Some things are best forgotten."

I pulled my hoof out just in time before Doubledose slammed shut the door. A yelp puckered my snout. My eyes burned. Without even looking where my hooves took me, I raced into the darkness. On and on I went.

A wailing wind stalked through the skeleton trees. Their leafless branches clattered above me. Misfit . . . misfit . . . misfit . . . they all seemed to say. I clamped my claws against my ears and kept running until my hooves refused to go any further.

With my chest ready to burst, I finally collapsed against the cemetery gates, clutching a cold iron bar in each claw. I sank to the ground. The soft squeal of bats and a few ghostly moans helped still my pounding heart. I closed my eyes and inhaled the welcome blackness.

BAAAAROOOOONGGG!!!BAAAAROOOOONGGG!!!

The Last Bells! My claws flew to my ears to still the deafening sound. Shifting my eyes back and forth, I scanned the darkness. The Demon Hours were about to descend. Could I race home in time? No way! I needed to find shelter for the next two hours.

Or join in with the demons!

Why shouldn't I join the wild monsters tonight? What did I have to lose? I could be as evil and monstrous as any of them. Couldn't I? Even if my father was a misfit, I would show that I wasn't. I was a true-blood troll. Wasn't I?

But when I stormed through the cemetery gates, my heart raced once again. Perhaps it would be better to "discreetly spy out the proceedings prior to advancing into the fray"—as outlined in the Junior Scare Patrol Manual. My tail twitched nearly out of control as I yanked open a rusted mausoleum door, and crept inside. My panting echoed off the damp decay surrounding me. I scooted a skull from beneath me, before I heard whimpering from a far corner.

"Who's there?" I demanded gruffly to cover my alarm. The jarring clamor of the Last Bells still tolled outside.

"Don't hurt me, demon!" cried out a withered voice. Its high-pitched squeak sounded like a gremlin.

I snarled, feeling my anger and confusion rise. "Grrrr! Th . . . that's right. I'm a demon! Go! Get out of here!"

With a snap of my teeth and my most gruesome growl, I chased the ancient gremlin out. As he stumbled past me into the cemetery, I detected a weak, soapy scent on him. Narrowing my eyes, I studied him more closely in the moonlight. Had I seen the old creature sometimes walking to school beside that bubble-blowing Newton from the O.M.O. class?

Snotfargle! What did I care if he was some mutant's granddad? I growled once more for good measure then secured the door.

A heartbeat of eerie silence. The Last Bells had ended!

An avalanche of howls and roars nearly buried me then. Yet even as my teeth chattered, I forced my claws down from my ears. My tail twitched uncontrollably. I snorted. I . . . I must not be scared. I could take them. I was Malcolm McNastee!

A sinister snarl sounded outside, then another, and another. There must be a pack of demons very near. I tried to quiet my raspy breath—only so I could watch undetected. Another high-lighted segment from the Junior Patrol Manual. I dared to peek through a hole created by a broken brick and missing mortar.

A long tail flicked back and forth before me. I caught a whiff of Sabertooth, but there were too many monsters stalking among the tombstones. Quickly their scents mingled together in a demon jumble.

My ears perked up. A snarl. Surely I'd heard that one before. But then more and more snarls drowned it out.

A whimper! Oh no! Indeed, I knew that sound very well.

"Don't hurt me, demons," the squeaky gremlin voice cried out for the second time tonight.

Surely they would spare a withered-up old gremlin. I bit down on my tongue. Even if I hadn't.

Teeth snapped outside. A spine-chilling death cry. I peeked out. Splashes of blood. I fell back as claws scraped against the mausoleum door, no doubt leaving bloody paw prints. Crashing back into the pile of bones, I huddled in the same corner as the gremlin I'd forced out. His slightly clean smell still lingered. I stuffed my claw into my mouth to keep from screaming.

My heart thundered in my chest. There was no way I was joining in the Demon Hours. I took a deep breath—very glad that I'd bolted the rusted door in place. This was no Fiendful Fiends recess mayhem.

CHAPTER THIRTEEN

*Monster Rule #55: Expect the unexpected, and then eat it for
lunch.*

FRANK'S TALE

The next morning, I cringed when I pulled on a pair of mud-
died boots, a wrinkled and tattered shirt, and hole-splat-
tered pants. I automatically reached for my comb, and then I
remembered. It drifted among the piranhas.

Last night after talking with Oliver, Georgina, and the others
in my class, we'd agreed to misfit teamwork. But since we didn't
exactly have a plan yet, we'd stay camouflaged in the expected
monster mode until we could figure it all out. Hadn't Witch
Picklepuss said that a monster's path isn't usually a straight one?

I pressed my fingers over my nostrils and unscrewed the
skin potion, which Pap had given me last night. With a squeeze,
I squirted a blob onto my arm.

"Ouch!" I jerked back. The concoction burned worse than a
dragon's kiss. I quickly rubbed the lotion off. The Moratorium
mixture had left a wrinkled brown scar. If only I could endure
the pain, this stuff might make me a monster shade of normal.

FROM the GRAVE

"You are more than monster enough!" The words spun me around.

"Granny?" I whispered, trying to silence my breathing. No response. Still I felt she was near. I shoved the skin cream into my top dresser drawer, grimacing only a little when some goop squirted onto a clean pile of shirts.

"Okay, Granny," I said, speaking to the empty room but believing she could hear. "My skin stays blue."

A crow cackled outside my window. It pushed off a bony branch, loop-de-looped once, and sailed away. If only my troubles would fly away as easily. With a honk, our O.M.O. bus lurched to a stop in front. Mr. Aldolfo waved up at me.

Pink, freckled skin like Mr. Aldolfo's would be as strange to me as the green skin they said I should have. Or Malcolm's deep orange or Ms. Hagmire's brown. I had to find a way to stay true blue and to stay in Uggarland!

I grabbed my newly tattered backpack and stepped into the hall. Taking careful aim with my appropriately mucked-up boots, I attempted to step on only squeakless floorboards. But, of course, I found too few in our well-maintained monster home. Oliver and I liked to play this game when we were little brats. We pretended that if we didn't make a sound, we were invisible. But a ten-hoof tall blue Frankenstein like me was far from invisible. Right now in these awful clothes, I felt like I glowed neon bright.

Nodding hello to Mr. Aldolfo, I stepped onto the bus. The driver slumped over the wheel as usual. I wondered if he scrunched up like that to make himself less noticeable. Perhaps it became second nature if a monster (a reformed monster) did it enough.

"Well, well, well. Look at the scumtwattle that just walked on."

A troll hoof tangled with my dirty boots. I tumbled to the

floor, banging my head against a seat brace. Malcolm! What was he doing on our misfit bus?

"Stay as far away from me as possible." He spat the words into my ear. "Your end time is coming as soon as I can make it, but don't tempt me to make it now!" He yanked me to my feet and shoved me toward the back. His red eyes seemed clouded. His green hair tuft droopy. I shuffled down the aisle quickly, only too ready to avoid him.

A gurgly whistle pulled my head up. Georgina flapped a short arm, beckoning me to join her. I glanced back at Malcolm. He sat down opposite Aldolfo and eyed a list in his claw.

"Put this rat trap in gear, Aldolfo. Three more losers left to pick up." Malcolm stomped a hoof on the floor, sending up a small shower of dust. "I want to get this bus duty over sooner rather than later." He slumped tiredly into a seat.

The bus pitched forward. I carefully maneuvered down the aisle to Georgina. She shifted her tail out of the way. I sat behind her and leaned forward. I couldn't stop myself from tucking my muddy boots from sight.

Pointing toward Malcolm, I asked, "What's he doing here?"

"Mr. Aldolfo told me that Principal Snaggle assigned him to bus duty. To make sure we stay in line. No more unmonsterly deeds even on the way to school."

"The principal's trying to be more thorough, huh?"

"I guess he knows he's running out of time. Like us. We have to do good or he doesn't look good." Georgina tilted her head back. Her moist breath tickled my ear. "And because we're almost out of time, that's why we have to go tonight."

"Go where?"

She cupped her claw around her mouth and lowered her voice to a whisper. "Exxillium. For the rescue."

"What!" Lowering my voice, I whispered to Georgina. "Last night we agreed to stay low and move slow. No escape plans!"

FROM the GRAVE

Malcolm stood at the front of bus, his eyes surveying every seat. They narrowed in on me. He pointed a claw at me and then drew it back to his own eye. Aldolfo slammed the bus to a stop for another pickup. Malcolm flopped down into the seat, barely managing to avoid landing in the stairwell.

"Watch out, you goon! Snaggle will hear about this."

Oliver limped on. I waved to him. He could barely walk. His wrappings encased him tighter than a tomb. With tiny steps, he tiptoed to the nearest seat and collapsed. I groaned to see him like that. But I needed to talk Georgina out of doing something crazy, so I stayed put. Aldolfo shifted and we rumbled on to our next pickup—whoever that might be. Our bus driver had trouble remembering the route, so it was a new schedule every day.

Georgina leaned close. "I know we agreed on misfit teamwork to prove we are monsters. And we didn't talk about escapes, but I think that's what we need to do. Rescue them."

I snaked my head into the aisle, making sure no others were listening or watching. All the monsters on the bus—except of course for Malcolm—were my friends. I would have trusted them with anything. I was one of them. Still I couldn't stop the fear creeping into my thoughts. Perhaps this was part of the process of becoming the monster the others wanted me to be.

"Rescue? What are you talking about? Did Exxillium fry your brain as well as your skin yesterday? We only talked about showing Uggarland that we misfits are already monster strong."

"And a rescue would prove that."

"It will prove we need to be sent to Exxillium—now!"

"We need to rescue Zelda . . ."

"She's been exiled! We can't do anything about it."

"You saw what it was like there for her. And she's not much older than us."

"Exactly! And we would be next, if we tried an Exxillium rescue. Look at me." I held out my ratty coat sleeves and pointed to my muddy boots. "I'm hanging in there until we think of the best plan. You should too. I've caused too much trouble already. I've . . . I've hurt a lot of people. And I don't want to hurt them worse by doing something stupid."

Georgina's eyes flamed. A gurgle rose up in her long throat. I leaned away from any possible spray. "But why was the first young monster to be exiled a female? A witch?"

I shrugged. "Bad luck for Zelda, I guess."

"Not just bad luck," muttered Georgina. "Too often witches get the blame when stuff goes wrong. It's easy to say their magic caused bad things to happen. But somehow none of the warlocks ever get punished, do they? All the more reason we should help Zelda."

"Okay, sure. She's gotten a raw deal, but let's take a little time to think about this Exxillium stuff."

Georgina gurgled again and shook her head. "No amount of time is going to help me, Frank. Do you think I can ever learn to breathe fire and stop leaking water? I can't. Well, not unless I stop drinking any water or stop breathing. Hmmm? Guess what will happen to me if I do that. I'll die!"

I hung my head and tapped my dirty boots together beneath the seat. I could hear clods of dried mud dropping to the floor. "Sorry. I didn't know."

"I am what I am. It's who I am." Georgina's large wings twitched. "And Zelda is who she is. I just hoped they'd let us hang around until we finished school."

"President Vladimir doesn't seem to care about giving us any more time."

"Lucky us. We'll go down in history along with Zelda, I guess. Unless . . ."

I didn't want to say it, but I did. "Unless we rescue her, you mean." I twisted a neck bolt tighter. "You're crazy to even think it. She's on Exxillium. Strictly off limits. And guarded by two scary Minotaurs—Goon One and Goon Two."

"I went back last night after we talked on the phone," Georgina whispered.

"Warts and wood toads!" Both my neck bolts buzzed. Malcolm tilted a pointy ear toward us. Trolls were known for their good hearing.

Oliver waved a tightly wrapped arm at me, motioning me to join him. I had to pretend not to see. I couldn't let my best friend be caught up in trouble like what Georgina proposed.

I leaned closer toward her. "No way you went back. You couldn't have."

The *thump, thump, thump* of her tail beat a fierce rhythm on the floorboards. "I may not be able to breathe fire, but my internal aerial-mapping talents are good. Really good. I seem to zap up info on locations, altitudes, and wind speed like breathing. It's all so natural for me."

Her voice quavered as she continued. "They put me in the misfit class in first grade because of all the times I spat out water instead of fire. They didn't give me any more chances. Not even one day in a Dragon Flight Dynamics class." Her eyes narrowed. "But I taught myself. I felt it all inside. I knew I could do it. I made up small tests for myself—flying from one gravestone to another in the cemetery. Blindfolded. Then I started going on longer and longer trips—without any maps."

Georgina paused. Her tail stopped tapping. "Once I've flown somewhere, I know exactly how to return there."

I paused, studying one of the jagged holes in my pants and the blue skin peeking through. "All that maneuvering stuff—it's really important to you, isn't it?"

"They call us misfits and say we don't belong. But we know. We know we've as much monster blood running through us as any of them. There are different ways to monster. If they'd only let us show them."

I sucked in a breath. Witch Picklepuss had said nearly the same words to me.

"Every monster knows The Rules get broken," whispered Georgina, "from time to time on the sly. They just don't want to admit it. That would ruin their vision of a perfectly run monster world. And we're the broken rules that are out there for every monster to see. They don't like that reminder."

"But you can't break this rule," I said. "You can't go back again. If they catch you, you'll be exiled for sure. Or . . . or even executed on the spot. Like the barbecued exiles the Minotaurs ate! You heard what Zelda said. They'd clip your wings. A drag-on's wings won't ever grow back."

"You think I don't know that?" Georgina's mouth puckered. Her eyes glistened. She stared through the bus window at the morning drear, as though she would find the answer etched in a bony skeleton tree's bark.

I ground a crumbling chunk of mud beneath my toe. More and more I was coming to believe there was no answer to monsters and misfits and exiles and rules. None with a happy ending for odd monsters out.

Georgina spoke in a forceful whisper. "I promised them."

"Them? I thought we were talking about Zelda. Only."

"And the troll. The one you were talking to. He begged me to get him back."

"The troll?" I groaned. "Did he, ah, tell you who he was?"

Georgina nodded. "We are their only chance. Zelda doesn't deserve an early death because she can't fly. And Mr. McNastee wants to be with his family again."

"I know. He hasn't even seen Nelly yet." A picture of Malcolm's little sister, flapping a pair of harpy wings and twirl-ing in a pink tutu, flashed before me.

"But if Malcolm ever found out we helped bring his dad back from Exxillium . . ." I peered up to the front of the bus. Malcolm perched in the aisle, busy surveying all us flunkies. I cupped a blue hand about my mouth before I whispered, "We will be the ones begging to be exiled."

Georgina gurgled. The thump of her tail rat-tat-tatted on the bus floor, like a monster march beat. "But who else will help them? This may be the last thing I do, but I have to try and save them."

I snorted. "Well, if we're going do a rescue, why stop with just Zelda and Mr. McNastee? Maybe that goofy Gooney wants to come back or the creature crawling in the sand like a turtle, or the gargoyle who wore fruit rinds for decoration."

"We'll start with two."

"Start?" I shook my head. "No, no, no!"

"These two want to return the most, from what I saw. Too many of the others were on the verge of imploding. I don't think we can help them. But if we develop a good enough plan with our first practice run, we could maybe try to rescue others."

"No, no, and absolutely no!"

Georgina gurgled and continued on like she'd not heard me. "I can't do it all on my own. You've always taken the lead for us—the odd monsters out."

I shook my now shaggy head. "You are totally crazy. We haven't finished learning all the Scare Patrol tactics. We don't know how to plan escapes or find hideaways. And we sure don't know how to cure a witch's fear of flying. I bet even an ancient witch like my Granny Bubbie wouldn't have had enough magic to pull all that off."

Right then, a tingle tickled my right hand. Okay, more than a tingle. A red hot burning I couldn't ignore. I turned up my palm. A green *X* glowed in the center of my blue hand. In the exact spot Granny Bubbie had held onto when she'd uttered the words, "That's the last of my magic."

Georgina shot me a strange look. "You okay?"

I clamped my hands together, fell back against the seat, and said no more for the rest of the bus ride to Fiendful Fiends Academy.

I'M NOT SURE what it was, but after my talk with Georgina on the bus, I hardly spoke a word to any of my classmates that day. Even Oliver. My right hand still pulsed where the *X* was etched so clearly now. I thought it would fade as the day went on, but it seemed to glow ever brighter and burn ever hotter. Just like the fear inside of me.

In my mind, I pictured Exxillium. Its haunted inhabitants kept floating past. Zelda, and Mr. McNastee, and even that looney Gooney. It was like I could feel it all again: the gritty sand; the bright, burning rays; the fresh air and endless blue skies. I saw myself there, growing ever more lonely. Missing my family, my home, all of Uggarland. And then in a flash, I saw myself implode—shattering into a bumbillion tiny pieces.

No way. There was absolutely no way I would ever return there. Not even for Zelda or Mr. McNastee. I couldn't risk losing what I had here. Even if they wouldn't let me be exactly what I wanted, I still wanted to stay. I pressed my pulsing right hand against my desk and vowed then and there:

I would become the monster they expected me to be.

By the midday break, my empty belly churned like the dungeon lava pits. But I knew it was mainly my jumbled thoughts causing the pains. If I was going to be a true-blood monster, I needed to start acting like one. Mayhem when appropriate. I stopped in mid-step on my way to the barfeteria. I curled up my bottom lip, squinted my eyes, and growled at any students passing by—especially those from my class.

"You feeling okay?" Oliver asked.

I had to do it. I snarled at my best friend and punched his arm hard.

Oliver's nearly covered-up eyes blinked rapidly. He rubbed his arm. "What is wrong with you?"

"Like you don't know. You saw Exxillium yesterday. I'm trying to change."

"And this is how?" Oliver kept rubbing his arm.

"Well, you're not exactly helping me. Why can't you find an answer in one of those banned books you like to read?"

"Don't you think I've tried?"

I didn't want to, but it was for my friend's own good. I slugged Oliver's other arm. "Guess you better try harder to stay out of my way 'til I figure it out."

"Guess so," muttered Oliver. He shuffled down the hall, cradling both his arms.

My neck bolts tightened. I'd had to do it. I just hoped he understood. I hunched forward as a painful jolt ran from my hand up my arm. Groaning loudly, I clomped down the hall.

For once Stan and Dan approached without a laugh. "Hey," warned Dan, rubbing his stomach, "don't eat the dingle curds in the barfeteria or you'll feel even worse. We shouldn't have. I don't think they were ripe."

"Unripe dingle curds can cause big trouble," said Stan. "If you know what I mean."

"Try to burp," said Dan. "That'll make us feel better. One, two—"

"*Uuuurp!*" Stan grinned at himself. "Ah . . . that did make me feel better."

Dan bopped his twin's forehead. "You were supposed to burp on the count of three, so we could do it together."

Stan knuckled his fist. "Ooow! Now you asked for it. This is going to hurt you worse than it's going to hurt me."

"OOOwww!" The combined voices of the gargoyle twins echoed down the school hallway. First Stan punched Dan. Then Dan punched Stan—which, of course, meant that each was punching himself.

I slumped against the rough stone wall, feeling much worse than if I had downed a whole bucket of unripe dingle curds. Principal Snaggle stalked the far end of the hall, and I spied Malcolm fast approaching as well. His angry face reminded me of the Minotaurs' take-no-prisoners approach. He looked to be in a particularly potent mood.

Quickly, I yanked open the door to the belfry stairs and slipped inside. The last thing I needed now was an encounter with either of those two monsters.

CHAPTER FOURTEEN

Monster Rule #91: Monsters relish the darkness, especially that within.

MALCOLM'S TALE

It was midday as I stamp-stomped down the crowded school hallway to the barfeteria. I saw Principal Snaggle perched at the far end. Normally, I would have scampered past all the whiny underclass monsters, toppling them to the floor for fun, and hurried to his side. Now though, I slowed my hooves and tugged on my re-tied shark tooth pendant. I was tired, confused, and frightened.

As I ambled on, two low-flying underclass ghosts hovered in front of me.

"Hey, I can't see through you, creeps! Move or go invisible." But the stupid haunts didn't fade away fast enough.

Bam! I ran smack into a tightly wrapped mummy. The creature squeaked. I recognized the pathetic misfit. Frank's friend, Oliver.

"Where's your loser buddy? Afraid to come to lunch in case he runs into me?"

"If . . . if you mean Frank," Oliver stammered. "I don't know where he's at."

I delivered a shin-crunching kick to Oliver's right leg.

"Ow!" He crumpled to the ground.

"Maybe you better go find him. So the two of you can hide out together."

I grunted. Messing up that loser hadn't given me any of the usual mayhem rush. No heady exhilaration. I rubbed my sleep-deprived eyes.

Biffle-buckets! Considering that I'd only had a few hours sleep in the mausoleum last night, of course I was tired. That's all.

I drummed my claw against my chest harder and harder—thinking, thinking. If Doubledose was afraid to tell me the truth of my dad's disappearance, I knew he'd not tell anyone else. If the real story was found out, Doubledose would be doomed—along with me and Nelly. Of that I had no doubt. So the only risky factor remaining was Frank. But how to do him in without drawing attention to me?

A familiar pat-a-tat-tat of claws on the school hall floor drew me from my thoughts and back to Fiendful Fiends Academy.

"Cat got your tongue, McNastee?"

Principal Snaggle padded toward me in the crowded hallway. His long tail flicked behind him. "Have you learned that human colloquialism in your Moratorium studies yet? It's really a rather monsterly saying, I think. And even though you do look totally lost in thought . . ." He slid a furry arm around my shoulders and steered me toward his office. "I need to talk with you again."

"But I haven't had lunch yet, sir."

"Ahhhh!"

Principal Snaggle stifled a yawn. His eyelids hung low. His left ear looked decidedly scuffed up. He patted at a fresh scratch on his chin and a bent whisker.

I snorted. Booger bandits! If I didn't know better, I'd think he'd spent the night stalking prey instead of sleeping. But there hadn't been any Scare Patrol scheduled for last night. I quivered. With a shaky claw, I tugged on my black leather vest. Remembering last night—a flicking tail, a familiar scent and snarl. Now I was being as goofy as Stan and Dan. Principals were some of the tamest monsters of all. They lived for The Rules.

"Ahhhhhh!" Principal Snaggle yawned again. His sharp fangs gleamed. "As I was saying, McNastee. Sorry about having you miss your lunch, but duty calls."

"Sir, if you're planning another trip for some of the misfits to Exxillium . . ." I paused and tried to suck in my pudgy belly. "I'd rather you find some other monster cadet to take 'em."

Principal Snaggle's thin lips creased into a crooked smile. "Didn't enjoy the excursion, McNastee? Can't say that I blame you. Never been there myself and never plan to go." He patted me on the back. "Don't fear. I'll find other ways to use you. Like the bus patrol this morning. How was that?"

"No problems, sir. I kept them all in line. No odd behavior to report. Well, other than the awful driving of Aldolfo. I'm surprised he hasn't rolled that bus and killed all of them by now."

"That would be a win-win, wouldn't it?"

I snorted.

"McNastee, I applaud your bravery for enduring the ride. I am quite fortunate to have a student like you. A true-blood student to assist me during these trying times."

"Yes, sir. Principal Snaggle, sir." I squirmed though when he called me a true-blood.

"Hmmm. I saw your name on the list for the next Scare Patrol on Frightday. That's only three days away. Coming up quickly."

"Yes. I'm leading the Junior Scare Patrol Team on a practice drill that night, sir."

"Most admirable, McNastee. But I'm afraid it's going to be called off this week. Predictions of a bad storm passing through from Moratorium into the Shadowlands. A Category twenty-one: Beyond Bad Horrorcane. Possibly even escalating to a Category twenty-five: Run for Your Lives Horrorcane."

"I hadn't heard, sir." I tried to shift away. I needed more rumination time. Alone. "I'll alert my squad, sir."

"Excellent!" Principal Snaggle tilted his chin up. His eyes studied the vaulted stone arch above the office doorway before he pushed me inside. His paw clenched my arm firmly, shoving me down into the chair. He shut the door. "Hmmm . . ." he purred, drumming his sharp nails on his whiskered chin. "I wonder if we aren't missing another opportunity to put the misfits in harm's way. I mean—to reform them. And, of course, bring recognition to Fiendful Fiends Academy and its illustrious principal." He patted his stuffed pet vulture.

I grunted.

"Come now, McNastee. You seem distracted. Surely a monster as clever as you can help me with this. I thought we could bounce a few ideas off each other. Evil begets evil, so they say." He bowed his head and locked his yellow eyes on me.

I dug a hoof into the encrusted dirt between the stones.

"Come. Come. Lunchtime is nearly over. I've a school to run." Principal Snaggle flicked his tail—back and forth, back and forth.

I tried to look away, but I kept seeing the other tail flicking back and forth in the cemetery darkness. My heart thundered in my chest again. I ground my hoof deeper between the stones.

"Really, McNastee!" Principal Snaggle huffed a fishy breath in my face. "So you've got nothing! How disappointing. I thought with all the on-the-job experience I've been giving you of late, that you would be ready to take the initiative for once. But it seems I'll have to devise the next malicious misadventure myself."

"Wait!" I snorted. I threw back my head, trying to clear my brain of last night's Demon Hours. "Let me think."

Principal Snaggle glanced at the gloomdial clock on his wall and raised his furry eyebrows.

Clutching the shark tooth at my chest, I rubbed its sharp edge. I must show that I wasn't a misfit. At last, under the principal's hypnotic stare, my monster wiles kicked into gear. I leapt from the chair. "I've thought of it!"

"Have you now," said Principal Snaggle, arching his back. "Do tell."

Leaning close I whispered, "A scavenger hunt for the misfits into the Shadowlands during the storm."

"My, my, my. Such wonderfully wily ways, McNastee. A young monster any father would be proud of."

I gulped. Even the principal's praise couldn't stop me from smarting at the mention of my father.

Principal Snaggle's lips slid up toward his slitted eyes. "You and I can see how silly the weather warning is. Blazing bunions! What's to become of this current generation if we don't put them in harm's way? It's only a bit of debris and havoc—which, of course, may last for days. Such a mega storm that even the most seasoned of scavengers wouldn't blunder into it. Why, of course, it's a perfect opportunity to test my struggling students."

I snorted. "To uh, prove they've, uh, changed."

"Truly changed," said Snaggle.

"And that they can follow orders," I added grinning. "Monster or die."

"Exactly," agreed Snaggle. "Either they brave a turbulent Shadowlands experience and show they are monsters. Or they run away, proving they're miserable mutants."

"Um, sir, a cautious monster isn't always a mutant," I mumbled, remembering my barricade last night inside the mausoleum.

"Pffft." Principal Snaggle waved his claw in the air. "Monster is as monster does, McNastee. We are drawn to mayhem like sloth beetles to the flames. Retreating misfits will certainly reveal their mutant natures amid the chaos. We'll be able to ship them to Exxillium ahead of schedule."

"If they make it back, sir." My tail twitched uncontrollably. My words sounded jittery as well. "I've heard whole houses can blow through sometimes. They say once a witch had a house land on her."

"Monster tales. Just monster tales for little tykes. We've all heard them." Principal Snaggle waved a sharp nail close to my snout. "Don't believe everything you hear. A tale or the truth. Monsters tend to mix the two up so frequently. But even if the witch did meet her end crushed beneath a bit of timber, what a gallant death. Don't you think?"

"Yes, sir." My head nodded so vigorously that my hair tuft bobbed down over my eyes. I envisioned Frank flattened beneath a house. My grin grew wider. "It sounds like a perfect plan."

"Of course it does. And you thought of it!" Principal Snaggle slapped me on my back. "A smart monster stays one step ahead. He leaves no room for error. No room for mishaps—that he doesn't intend."

"I second that," I said. And to be doubly prepared, I could add additional danger to the excursion for one particular misfit. Very grave danger. I chuckled at my own lame joke, but I cut it short—remembering that looney Gooney on Exxillium and all his goofy humor. Snotfargle! Misfit and monster. The lines kept blurring behind my tired and much-more-than-normally bloodshot eyes.

Principal Snaggle flicked his tongue across his sharp teeth. "No need to alarm anyone about the weather. I'm sure I can convince any concerned parents that it's all in the best interests of their children. And if by some fluke of nature, these misfits do somehow succeed—just think. What an extraordinary principal

I'd be then. Perhaps they'll want to nominate me for Principal of the Year again. On the other claw, a team of reformed misfits, meeting an untimely end in a valiant monster scavenger effort, would reflect quite well on their trendsetting principal also. It's another win-win for me. As it should be."

I nodded again. Somehow I'd make doubly sure Frank's destiny would not be in doubt. And neither would mine be. Frank would not return from the Shadowlands. My family and I would still be the true-blood trolls that we'd always been known to be.

My plan would be a win-win also. I just had to devise a dastardly backup plan to ensure Frank's most horrible end. That was all.

CHAPTER FIFTEEN

Monster Rule #913: A well-educated monster knows not to ask any questions.

FRANK'S TALE

That afternoon, Ms. Hagmire shouted out another review lesson for the upcoming Monster Achievement Test. But my eyes were glued on the twists and turns of Oliver's tightly tied mummy wrappings. Even though I knew this was for the best, I couldn't fathom Oliver like this. No pile of dingy strips puddled at his feet. No wrinkled, nut-brown face exposed for all to see. No banned books stuffed in his desk.

"Let's begin," said Ms. Hagmire in her loud, grating voice. "Today we will take a practice exam to help you prepare for the Monster Achievement Test—which is coming very soon!"

Only one weak groan rose from our out-of-sorts students. I rubbed my jaw. This didn't seem like my classroom.

"Now," said our teacher, "clutter up your desks. Quickly! Leave as little work space as possible."

I shook my head. My mind melted amid clutter. I'd totally fail the test if I was surrounded by messiness. I cringed as I dumped my backpack contents on my desk. Hopefully I could at least elbow some of it to the side when Ms. Hagmire wasn't looking.

With her tail dragging down the aisles behind her, our teacher threw out the test papers. I scrambled to catch one as it floated my way.

"Remember," said Ms. Hagmire, pointing to the classroom gloomdial. "This test is timed. When the gloom reaches three, time will be up. Except for the Growling portion of the exam, which will be conducted separately."

Newton sniffled loudly.

"You've been skulking about all morning," said Ms. Hagmire, baring her teeth. "Quite unmonsterly."

Newton wiped his eyes. "My grandpa . . . he didn't make it home last night."

I gulped. I thought Newton had been upset about having to monster up today—no more bubble blowing or lemon-fresh scent. But it was much worse. We all knew what it meant when a monster didn't come home. The Demon Hours.

Our teacher cleared her throat and pushed up her spectacles. She started to reach out a claw toward Newton but quickly pulled it back. "Tsk! Tsk!" she muttered. "Demons will be demons." She swallowed. "Get started!"

I gave Newton a reassuring nod. He sucked in a sniffle and picked up his test.

With a sigh, I turned my eyes to my test as well. Making sure Ms. H wasn't watching, I scooted aside a pile of crumbled papers, a half-eaten Gurglenut Chewie, and one of Spidey's eight-legged relatives that had crawled into my bag. There, that was a little better. I turned over the test and scanned the questions.

MONSTER ACHIEVEMENT TEST
(MISFIT VERSION)

Write all answers as sloppily as possible. No corrections are allowed but cross outs are encouraged. Extra credit given for smudges. Points will be deducted for neatness.

MATH

An elderly vampire bit twenty-seven people on the first night. The second night he bit only fourteen. How many will he bite on the third night, after having his false teeth repaired?

DECEIT

Which of the following lies would work best when told to a parent who has discovered the family dinner devoured ahead of time?

A. "I saw my brother's pet iguana wolfing down the Crud Egg Casserole."

B. "I only eat raw Crud Eggs, remember."

C. "What Crud Egg Casserole? Buuurp!"

FRIGHTENING

Match the classic attack sound to the monster:

1. Arooooooooooo!   _ Yahooligan

2. Grrrrrroooooowl!   _ Werewolf

3. Yawooooooooo!   _ Banshee

HISTORY

Match the following famous monsters to the event associated with them.

1. Gingus the Gargoyle   _ Instituted the midnight fly-by

2. Tarton Colossal   _ Conquered the wild swamplands

3. Sabrina Bloodstone   _ With one foot, smashed the city of Monstropolis

FROM the GRAVE

Whew! Not too tough but the pages went on and on. I dipped my pen in the newt's blood ink and began. The gloom went by too quickly.

"Time is almost up," yelled Ms. Hagmire, as the clock's shadow edged close to three.

I hurried to finish the last question, an essay about the best methods for sneaking up on children. With a flourish of newt blood, I signed my name and cringed as I smudged my signature.

Turning about in my seat, I studied all my classmates. I was proud of them for trying their best to meet the requirements at least for now, until we figured out an alternative to save us from Exxillium. I shuffled my scuffed up boots. Wasn't that the best plan?

Vanya sat slumped in her desk chair, attired in scuffed-up boots and ratty clothes. I couldn't see a trace of sparkly makeup and certainly no tiara or jewelry. But it looked like she'd been crying her Ogre eye out.

Georgina, too, looked grim. She cradled her dragon snout in a claw and stared blankly ahead. A rusted bucket sat on the floor next to her, ready for any watery mishaps. She had to understand that blending in was our best bet for staying in Uggarland right now. But could she ever blend in enough—and keep breathing? Was I asking the impossible for her? I guessed she was still thinking about Exxillium.

Stan and Dan, always ready with a joke, both sat tombstone quiet. It was like watching a sizzling pot of entrails—waiting for the first one to explode. I feared they couldn't stay quiet for long. Not without doing themselves permanent damage anyway.

Directly behind them sat Ratsmelda Katomb. She was a third grade hunchback who'd been born without a hunch. Today instead of sitting up straight like usual, she was bowed over by a noticeable lump on her back. I gave her a thumbs-up when she looked my way, but she only squirmed in her chair, trying

Olivia Reeg

to find a comfortable position. She seemed so little to already be saddled with such a heavy load.

Behind me, Bianca Fantasma, a fifth grade ghost who was usually too frightened to even appear, hovered in the last row. Her misty shape hid mostly beneath her desk—only the top of her head and her wary eyes peeked out. Her nervous hiccupps echoed through the classroom. Why must every ghost like haunting?

The green *X* in my right hand glowed. I shoved it into my tattered pants pocket but it still pulsed, sending a painful jolt up my arm. Perhaps I'd asked too much of my classmates. My good intentions might well be their undoing. Perhaps trying to conform would make them as miserable as Exxillium. Could the pressure to stay in Uggarland cause one of them to implode?

"Oliver," commanded Ms. Hagmire. "Collect the papers. Quickly, quickly!"

But Oliver could barely move with his too-tight wrappings. I lowered my head, unable to watch my best friend's painful walk. By the time he finally made it to the front of the room, I dared to glance up. But I shouldn't have.

"Ooops!" he cried, tripping over Georgina's tail.

"OW!" Georgina moaned. Her snout curled up and a loud gurgle filled the room.

"What's going on here?" said Ms. Hagmire, hovering over the two.

"Watch out!" I warned, after hearing the potent gurgle. Our teacher stood in the direct line of fire. Ms. Hagmire let out a most unmonsterly squeal. "Stop," she cried. "No. Sneezes!"

But her warning was too late.

"Ahhhh . . . *KER-Whoosh!*" Georgina showered a hefty gush of snotty spray.

"What! Oooooo! Bat boogers!" Ms. Hagmire scrambled about like a warted wiggle worm drenched with salt. "Look what you've done!" She glared at Georgina then searched like a crazed harpy through the large burlap bag beside her desk. She tossed out a box of Crispy Critters, a bottle of Toe Nail Fungus Fumes, and a strange looking paper-wrapped bar before she pulled out a large, ratty towel. With rapid strokes she rubbed her dripping skin with the towel. Scrubbing and rubbing herself dry.

All my classmates watched in stunned silence. This rattled and totally out-of-control Ms. Hagmire was not familiar to us. Even though she was a swamp monster, she seemed gigantically upset about getting wet. Maybe though, she was just embarrassed about being drenched with dragon drool in front of the class. She continued scrubbing so furiously it looked as though she might scrape some of her scaly skin away.

By the time she'd finished her crazed toweling off, her breath came in short gasps. Her wiry hair stood on end. Her spectacles were clouded with fog. And her usually brown skin glowed a jangleberry red. My neck bolts buzzed. This would be trouble.

A giggle—not muffled well—broke the silence. I'm not sure if it was Stan or Dan, but too late they each slapped a hand over the other's mouth.

"You!" Ms. Hagmire pointed at the gargoyle. "To detention." Next she pointed at Georgina. "And this water breathing dragon who enjoys spraying teachers. Really! A dragon without a drop of fire. Disgusting."

Even though Georgina's eyes were hooded with heavy dragon lids, I saw some tears leak out. They dripped down into the puddle on the floor at Ms. Hagmire's feet.

Oliver unwound two strips from his mouth. "Georgina didn't do it on purpose."

"And you! A mummy who can't keep his wrappings on will most certainly go to detention too."

My neck bolts buzzed. My hand glowed hot with Granny's *X*. My mind whirled with 'monster is and monster isn't.' We misfits would never be able to reform. Shouldn't have to reform. I leaped from my desk, threw back my head and wailed like a cornered Wilderbeast. "Nooooo!"

Ms. Hagmire's thin, dry lips twisted up. Her sneer tipped her eyes into slits. "That sad attempt at a growl, Monster Gordon, has earned you a spot in the dungeon as well. Get out of here. Before I send the entire class!"

CHAPTER SIXTEEN

Monster Rule #71: Torture is often a necessary component of monster education.

MALCOLM'S TALE

I licked my lips when I walked through the dungeon door with two other student guards. There was Frank, surrounded by a few of his misfit pals.

"Time to string 'em up," said the ancient dungeon monitor with a wave of his paw.

"You just made my day, dork dung!" I shoved Frank against the slimy dungeon wall and tied his hands securely behind his back. Then I wound a chain around his barrel-chested midsection.

I huffed as I turned the pulley crank. "You've put on a few pounds. All in your fat behind it looks like."

With each crank, Frank rose higher up the wall. I raked him across a particularly sharp stone.

"Hey, Malcolm," he said, through gritted teeth, "your hair sprout looks decidedly limp today. Something frighten you?"

"Only the thought of having to spend more time with you." I secured the rope and poked Frank's gut as I passed by. Then I lent my knowledgeable assistance to my fellow two guards. In short order, we had the misfits suspended and squirming. All except for Georgina, who was much too large. Instead, we strapped her to the monster stretching apparatus. Her long neck was pulled tight. Her arms and feet were splayed to the sides, and her tail we secured with an anvil.

She gasped as I tugged her another notch tighter.

"Hope everyone's as uncomfortable as possible," I said with an insulting arm salute.

Frank jerked his head toward me. "The real torture is still seeing you."

I snorted, intent on proving myself. "That's your whole problem. You pale when confronted with pure monsterness, like me." At least that line seemed to shut the odd bat up for a while. All of them.

"Lights out," said the monitor, an old Sabertooth who slept more than he supervised. That's why student guards were needed so often. "Hurry up," he croaked, ready to bar the door.

I saluted and snuffed out the wall torch. Blackness devoured the scene.

"Ahh," said Frank through the dark. "Finally. I can't see your face."

Blasted mutant! I slammed shut the dungeon door and slid the bolt in place. If only snuffing out Frank's spark would be as easy as extinguishing the torch.

BEFORE THE FINAL gong of the school day, I slunk down the nearly deserted hall to my classroom. My ears pointed up on alert. My eyes darted in all directions. I pretended I was on a Scare Patrol Mission—ever vigilant. But deep inside I knew who I was really on the lookout for, and he was no human freak. Nor a misfit either.

A few minutes later, I dropped into my seat. I snorted happily—pleased at making it back to class with no Principal

Snaggle encounter. I lifted my left arm, taking a long armpit whiff. I grinned. Particularly potent. At least guard patrol duty had some bonus benefits.

"Looks like you are proud of yourself." Mr. Wartwood slid beside me. He held a pile of papers in his skinny arms.

"Monsters shouldn't be modest, right Mr. Wartwood?"

"I'm sure no one's ever accused you of that, Malcolm. You have quite the bravado."

Ghoulbert leaned into the aisle. "I wouldn't let him say stuff like that about you."

"He means I can boast about my boldness and bravery with the best of them."

Mr. Wartwood slipped his pointed tongue through his closed lips. His eyes gleamed. "Something like that. Here are the handouts you missed while on guard duty. They are all due by tomorrow."

I groaned. "Never thought I'd say it, but I'll be glad when Mrs. Eerie returns from maternity leave. I'll even look at pictures of her newest, nasty gremlin. At least, she's a teacher who hates to grade papers. No papers mean no homework."

"Tut, tut," said Mr. Wartwood, shaking his triangular head. "Monsters are made to endure. To strive toward the ultimate goal."

"I think your goal and mine are two different things," I said as the final gong sounded. I stuffed the papers into my properly ratty backpack and took a step toward the door.

"I am intent on helping you be the best monster you can be," said Mr. Wartwood. "I do speak from experience."

"Your time at B.A.D., you mean?"

Mr. Wartwood's forked tongue slipped in and out of his thin lips before he spoke. "Lots of valuable training there with your grandmother."

I tapped my hoof into the stone floor. Grandma Ooogle

was all the more reason to prove my true McNastee self by concocting Frank's demise.

"Oh yeah, remember that assignment you gave us, Mr. Wartwood? To come up with the ten best methods to do an opponent in?"

"Yes, of course. The one you've failed to hand in yet."

"Yeah. I need a little help with it. Like if I wanted to be doubly sure an opponent was a prime target. How might I do that?"

"Well, Malcolm, do you mean a human or a monster? There are rules about annihilating another monster, outside of the Demon Hours. Very serious rules."

I curled my tail up tight. "Not a human in a scare patrol. More like, you know, an arena-type situation. The Minotaur labyrinth duels. I'm a big fan of Deadalus Bullfull."

Ghoulbert stood at my side, waving his hand in the air. "Or the Soultice Monsterator Games. When the strongest monsters come from all over to compete. My uncle Brutus made it into the finals one year. He's one rough and tough . . ."

I elbowed Ghoulbert. No need to let the goon—I mean, my sort-of friend—keep running his big mouth off. More than likely it would only lead to trouble. "Yeah, like that. Any ideas?" I paused and pressed my shark tooth against my chest.

Mr. Wartwood flicked his tongue. "You do seem intent on this assignment. But since I don't want to spoil your chance to do some proper research, my advice is to consult the *Ultimate Mayhem Encyclopedia*. I'm sure you can find a copy in the school slybrary. Mrs. Rathmite should be able to assist you. Fiendful Fiends Academy is quite fortunate to have a slybrarian of her expertise."

I grunted. Just what I needed. Another book to look at. Mr. Wartwood may have worked at B.A.D., but I could tell he wasn't going to share any secrets he'd learned there. Somehow his guarded answer made me all the more determined. After all, actions spoke louder than words. Specifically, diabolical actions. Specifically, diabolical actions to destroy Frankenstein Gordon. Actions I would have to devise on my own to prove I was a true-blood troll.

CHAPTER SEVENTEEN

Monster Rule #11: Magic matters.

FRANK'S TALE

When school ended, I scurried out the main door. Even with my 'monster mode' plan in action today, four of us had ended up in detention. Didn't we at least get one free pass for trying? All my classmates had suffered trying to monster up. How much longer could any of us hold up as reformed misfits?

For sure, I needed some thinking time. But when I was trying to slink away, Oliver grabbed me in the courtyard. His tightly re-wrapped fingers clamped about my wrist.

"You limping?" I asked.

Oliver shrugged. "A little bit. Guess I got overstretched in the dungeon."

His slender fingers released their hold of my arm. Like the rest of him, they looked much too fragile. No bulk or brute force with Oliver. I was afraid he'd crumble faster than a dried up poop plop. I needed to keep him out of trouble.

"Georgina's looking for you," he said.

"Rats blood! I don't want to see her. And you can tell her that for me."

"Okay." Oliver held up his hands. "Don't run over me like road kill. I'm just delivering the message."

"Sorry." I ground my teeth and took a step away.

"Hey!" Oliver's voice stopped me. It's not easy to walk away from a best friend, even if he didn't understand all that was going on. "Where did you disappear to at lunchtime?"

I tried to snarl at him but couldn't. "None of your business where I was."

"You still intent on reforming?" Oliver tried to catch up with me, but he could only take minced steps in his super-tight strips. He stumbled and fell.

I grunted but didn't help him to his feet. "Tell Mr. Aldolfo I won't be riding the bus tonight."

"Why? Where are you going?" Oliver's voice cracked.

I didn't answer. I knew monster eyes spied on us. I stooped to pick up a rock. Ms. Hagmire stood under the stone archway into the school. Her eyes froze me with their flinty glare. Monster or die, they seemed say. With a growl, I threw the stone at a young ghoul. I couldn't hurt my friend anymore today. It thudded against his backpack and sent the small monster toppling.

Oliver moaned, as he righted himself. "This is who you're gonna be from now on, Frank?"

"I'm being a monster. Mayhem when appropriate. It's all I thought about when we were strung up today in the dungeon. Don't try to help him, Oliver. Ms. Hagmire's watching. She'll report back to Principal Snaggle. Monster up. So we can still stay here in Uggarland."

"Maybe," said Oliver, pulling away, "I won't want to stay. Not if we have to change so much."

"Not so much—just enough. For now, anyway. Until we figure out a better plan." I hoped.

"I'm thinking nobody's figured it all out yet." Oliver yanked a strip from around his eyes.

I glanced back to where Ms. Hagmire stood. "Don't let her see you!" I reached to rewrap my friend, Oliver jerked away. He stumbled onto the misfit bus.

"Snotfargle!" I yelped. The pain in my hand throbbed worse than ever. Granny's magic was as agonizing as it was confusing. I pushed past a trio of barking werewolf cubs. My right arm shot forward, pulling me down Phantom Street. Toward exactly where I didn't want to be. Granny Bubbie's house on Mushington Way.

WITH MY SENSES muddled by my achy hand, I'd forgotten about walking past Malcolm's apartment building on my way to Granny's. When I spied Nelly playing in the apartment courtyard, I knew I needed to hide fast or risk drawing Malcolm's attention. He might already be home from school.

I slid behind the overgrown jangleberry bushes. But I was too late.

"Frankie! Frankie! I see you! Boo!" Nelly jumped up and down.

Blasted wizard warts! Everyone in Uggarland must have heard Nelly's high-pitched greeting. I held a finger to my lips and hurried to her side.

"Boo," I said softly. "Now it's your turn to hide." But I planned to be the one to disappear. I scanned the apartment windows for a sign of Malcolm. I had strict orders from him to stay away from Nelly. Or else. Plus, after last night's call and the revelation about his dad—not to mention our dungeon encounter today—I wasn't ready to meet Malcolm all alone.

"No more hidey-boo," said Nelly. "Let's play dress-up. Here put this on." Nelly handed me a reptilian sleeve trimmed with swamp moss. "You be swamp monster. I fall in water. You save me." Nelly pretended to fall back into the swamp. "Help! Help! Help! I'm dwowning!"

"Shhhhh." I pulled Nelly up. "There. You're all saved. No more yelling." I thought I'd seen a face at the window. "I've got to go."

"Where you goin'?" Nelly petted a furry, spotted sleeve.

I ground my teeth again and collapsed beside Nelly and all her mismatched costume parts.

"My Granny Bubbie's house."

"Oh." Nelly looked thoughtful. "I wish I had a granny. Mine gone."

"I know. Both my grannies are gone now, too."

"Oh." Nelly nodded knowingly. "And my daddy is gone. Is your daddy gone? Like my daddy?"

I shook my head and tried to swallow, but it felt as though I'd taken a too-big bite of goober hardtack. A picture of exiled Roary McNastee flashed before my eyes.

"My daddy gone," said Nelly. "Forever."

"Sorry." If only she knew how really, really sorry I was.

"Here." Nelly handed me a furry sleeve. "A present. For your daddy, Frankie." Her round troll eyes beamed up at me.

My neck bolts twisted then. Tight. Tight. Tighter. My mouth clamped shut. All I could do was nod and stuff the sleeve into a pocket of my baggy, dirty pants. Then with lumbering Frankenstein steps, I clump-clomped the last block to Granny Bubbie's.

I TORE AWAY the cobwebs guarding the cellar door. Even after all these years since Granny's death, my family was still undecided on what to do with her house. Pap wanted to sell it, but witches' houses too often came booby-trapped with multitudes of insufferable spells. Plus, the housing market had fallen into a slump in the last year. With the monster economy in a nosedive, it created even more pressure on young monsters to contribute. I remember one of President Vladimir's campaign promises, "Misfits suck the life from our failing economy. I will put them out of their misery before they make each of our lives a misery, too." The hordes had cheered wildly when they heard that promise.

As I reached for the cellar door, too many memories threatened to surface. I'd say monsters in general aren't exactly sentimental. Especially the brute species like trolls, Bigfoots, and such. But with countless years of intermarrying among the species, more variations had evolved among the creatures. It was difficult to predict which of the monster genes would be dominant. I guessed Mam's mixed genes contributed to her sappiness. She shrieked relentlessly whenever she even thought of parting with Granny Bubbie's home and things. Even though Granny's witch genes had basically skipped over her, Mam had a keen respect for magic.

She'd given me permission to hang out at the house whenever I needed a break from Ghoulbert or other stuff. I guess she knew the special connection me and Granny Bubbie had shared. Perhaps she even suspected that Granny had passed on the last of her magic to me. Whatever that meant. I still wasn't sure. I worried that it only meant more trouble.

I'd always loved coming here to Granny's. It was a place of safety. A place of welcome. Of acceptance. But today I'd been dragged here. Against my will. Today I feared what awaited me within the cellar depths.

Taking a deep breath, I yanked hard on the rusted handle. On the third tug, the heavy door yielded. Bending low, I maneuvered through the opening, careful not to let the door bang down on my head as I descended the stairs. My head was flat enough already.

The cold dampness sent a refreshing shiver snaking down my backbone. A welcome sensation after all the stinging pain I'd endured from my hand today. Still, I gasped, caught off guard by a tangle of cobwebs that ensnarled my head with my next step. I swiped at the invisible threads and blinked. My blue eyes weren't the best as far as night vision went.

"Oooof!" I sputtered, bumping the edge of Granny's large worktable. Finally, I made out the dim outlines of the space. On the table, I felt a lumpy candle in its holder and a flame sparker next to it. I flicked the gritty sparker switch and cupped the flame in my hand. Touching the flame to the candle's wick, I watched as the cellar's objects stepped forward into the light.

The green X etched on my palm glowed bright in the cellar gloom. The stinging pain from it pulsed from my hand, up my arm, and exploded behind my eyes. I pressed my hand to my forehead. The pain eased as Granny's image floated before my closed eyes.

Opening them, I called out, "Granny! Are you here?" How I wanted her to recite a spell, make triangle worms squirm in reverse, hear her cackle—just one more time. I wanted to be that same little Frankie Prankie whose frown she could change into squeals of delight with a simple peek into her magic cupboard.

But there was only silence.

"Snotfargle!" I said with a stomp. The dusty table rattled with the vibration.

Another red-hot shot of pain engulfed my hand. "Oww!" I cried, doubling over. The green X glowed more vividly. It pulsed with each heartbeat, growing brighter and brighter—until it outshone even the candle on the table.

"This is your magic, Granny. Isn't it?" My whispered words hung in the musty air. As if in answer, my glowing hand quivered and wrenched me to the right. Beads of sweat dripped from my wide forehead. I struggled to pull my hand back. To take control. But the more I tried to pull it back the more the pain increased. I feared that if the pain reached my heart, I would implode long before being sent to Exxillium!

"What do you want, Granny?" I whispered. "What?"

In answer, my hand yanked me from the chair, and I crashed to the floor. I lay sprawled. My face pressed into the cold, damp grit. The fingernails of my right hand dug into the dirt, tugging me forward. Tugging me toward the cupboard. My left foot bumped the table leg. The candle clattered down beside me, extinguished. A gray fog swallowed me up. But still my hand dragged me across the floor.

When I reached the cupboard, I rose up like a stiffened vampire ascending from a coffin. Prying open the cupboard doors, I grimaced when splinters bit into my fingers. A creaky cackle erupted from the rusty hinges. The doors swung open.

A pulsing green glow—much like the glimmer from my hand—encircled a leather-bound book in the center of the cupboard. I recognized the battered volume as Granny's spell book. I'd seen her consult it numerous times.

The clasp, which held it shut, glowed green as well. My right hand hovered above the clasp, summoned to it like a sloth beetle to a flame. My hand lowered of its own accord, pressing tight against the glimmering clasp.

With a shudder, I tore the lock away. The book tumbled to the floor. I stumbled back to the table and grabbed the extinguished candle. Even with the bright radiance from my hand, I needed more light to locate the dropped spell book and read it. I groped for the flame sparker on the tabletop.

"Snotfargle! Where did it go?" As I fumbled about, the light from my right hand intensified. The heat sparking from it increased. I moaned. Fire shot from my hand!

Suddenly the candle burst into flame.

"Rat splat!" I cried. "Did I just do that?" My right hand hovered above the flame. The fire from the candle linked to the X in my palm.

From the Grave

"Granny," I screamed. "What's happening to me? I've become a monster flame thrower!"

I slowly pulled my hand away from the candle. The candle stayed lit, but the fire radiating from my hand grew fainter. With a big breath, I blew it out. Only the X remained. My blue skin looked the same. No charring or burned flesh.

Gasping, I collapsed into the righted chair. With my shaky left hand, I reached for the burning candle. Slowly I lowered my fingers into the flame.

"They're not burning!" A sliver of flame, however, caught my sleeve, singeing it. I quickly pulled my hand away.

The fire itself then wasn't enchanted. Perhaps Granny's magic had given me this gift of fire. But had it also bewitched my skin so that it couldn't burn? Or was I fireproof because my skin was blue? Like a Bigfoot's fur could repel water.

I held my shaky right hand above the table, willing the heat to return. Slowly the glow lit up the tabletop.

"Warts and wood toads! This is monster amazing!" Breathing deeper, I tried to turn up the heat, gathering energy from my veins.

Whoosh! A small flame sparked, charring the dry wood. Snatching my hand back, I blew out the fire in my palm.

"Whoa, Granny! This is way better than turning into a toad. But way dangerous. A controlled fire is a safe fire, right?"

I heard a squeak behind me. A fat black rat jumped from the cupboard and landed with a plop on the floor beside Granny's spell book. "Scram!" I cried, shooing the critter away before he started gnawing the book to shreds. The giant fur ball hissed at me, showing sharp teeth. I aimed a flame its way. With a swish of its long tail, it scurried behind the cupboard.

A hint of roasted rat wafted up as I lifted the ancient book. I noticed some earlier nibbling by the rodent, but for the most part, the spell book looked sound enough. I carefully held it up to the candlelight. Without any aid from me, the book proceeded to open. My neck bolts buzzed as I read the text:

Overcoming a fear of flying.

In the margin were Granny's scribbled words. "Winging It for Dummies."

"No way!" I exclaimed, stomping my Frankenstein-size feet. The rat hiding inside the cupboard squealed.

"I don't understand any of this, Granny," I muttered, sitting back down. "Not my fire powers or this spell of yours. Is this the cure for Zelda?"

Suddenly, a wind rushed through the cellar. A bat flapped past my nose. A bat flying upside down. The creature flew past the black cellar wall and paused. When it darted away, a vision materialized in the darkness. I knew without a doubt this was Granny's magic.

Zelda and Mr. McNastee, clinging to a giant gloomdial. They clawed desperately to hang on, but they couldn't. First Mr. McNastee dropped into the black void surrounding them, followed by Zelda. The teen witch's scream echoed against the cellar walls. I gasped.

"They're almost out of time, Frankie." The words floated through me as the vision faded away. It was Granny Bubbie's voice—of that I was certain.

I clutched the opened spell book to my chest. "You said I was monster enough, Granny. But this seems more madness than monster. How can I help them escape Exxillium and not end up there myself?"

"Monster is as monster does," she replied.

I moaned. My voice stammered. "You're speaking in riddles. Monsters can't do whatever they want. We just went over The Rules in school today."

FROM the GRAVE

A cold wind whistled through the splintered boards of the cellar door. It wrapped about my ankles like icy shackles.

"The Rules were originally written to preserve and to protect. Now too many of them do harm. Not good for monsters." Granny's final words floated away, up the dark stairway. "Don't follow the pack into oblivion."

"Wait, Granny! Come back! I don't understand."

The wind outside stopped. Only silence kept me company now.

I took a deep breath. My right hand no longer glowed with the burning X. Only the spell book itself glowed.

The spell for transforming Zelda seemed to hover above the page, drawing my eyes to its every word. Zelda deserved a chance to flee Exxillium. But who knew if the spell would even work. Plus, Georgina wanted to help Mr. McNastee escape too. That seemed pure craziness.

Then I thought of Nelly's pleading eyes and her sad words: "My daddy is gone."

Gone—and not returning, without help. Without some magic.

I pushed myself up from the rickety chair, still holding the book tight to my chest. Georgina and me had everything to lose with an Exxillium rescue attempt—our friends, our families, our lives. Or perhaps we'd been fated to lose it all along—just by being born misfits.

I shook my head and repeated Granny's words, "Monster is as monster does." The door leading to Granny's kitchen creaked open. A stale waft of roasted mouse ears and singed vulture talons tickled my nose. Granny's potion ingredients still smelled plenty potent.

I grinned. "Okay. Okay, Granny. I get it. Scare or be scared."

Before this moment, my neck bolts had squeezed tight. My hand had erupted in flame. My heart and my head had threatened to explode. Every blue bit of me had twisted in agony—was I truly monster enough?

But now, the pain and confusion had gone. I took a deep breath. I knew what I had to do. Whether it scared the bezzelbugs out of me or not. Or even whether I totally understood why.

I had fire starter magic. I had fireproof blue skin. And I had Granny's encouragement to help light the way.

With one quick rip, I tore a ragged scrap of material from my brother's hand-me-down shirt and marked the page. I stamp-stomped up the stairs with the spell book clutched in my hands. I propped the book up on Granny's kitchen table and carefully studied the spell. The spell that might free Zelda from Exxillium. The spell that might lead me to my doom.

CHAPTER EIGHTEEN

Monster Rule #49: Commit your enemy's smell to memory or you'll soon not smell anything at all.

FRANK'S TALE

I had spent the remainder of the afternoon memorizing the spell and collecting the few ingredients listed in the recipe. Luckily, Granny's cupboard still contained almost all the necessary ingredients: a vat of fermented toadstool gills, a pouch of dizzy bug eyelids, and a crock of dingdang dung. The dung had dried up from not being sealed properly. I added a few drops of sludge water and stirred carefully. The dung stunk more profoundly than when fresh.

The final ingredient would have to be obtained from Zelda herself.

Later that evening, I called Georgina from the hall phone. Hunching over, I whispered, "It's a go for tonight. Meet me in the cemetery at midnight as planned. I've got the potion ready for Zelda. And a new secret weapon, if we need to use it." I shuddered thinking about the Minotaurs, Goon One and Goon Two. My final words squeaked out. "And whatever we do, we have to make it back here before the Demon Hours descend at 1:33 AM."

Georgina agreed with a gurgle.

I'd made one more call then—to Oliver. Lately I'd treated him like scumtwattle. I figured if something did happen to me, I wanted him to know he was the best friend a blue Frankenstein could ever have.

"This doesn't seem like a good idea," he said after hearing the rescue plan.

"Probably not."

"You're gonna do it anyway, right?"

"Scare or be scared."

"I thought you wanted to blend in and think up a better, safer plan."

"Yeah, I thought so too. Only there's no time for that. Not for Mr. McNastee and Zelda anyway."

Oliver paused. I could almost hear him unwrapping another layer of strips. "I want to help, Frank."

"No way!" My words were louder than I intended. I couldn't let Oliver join me on this dangerous trip. Georgina, even without fire, could handle herself well enough. Plus, we needed her to help fly us there and back. But I'd not be the cause for my best friend's end.

I cupped my hand around the phone and whispered. "You're just too fragile for an escape attempt. And with all your wrapping—you can't move anyway. But, um, thanks. Really."

I hung up then, before Oliver could say anything. 'Cause I knew it wouldn't take much more to convince me to call it all off.

I HURRIED THROUGH my supper (mac and sleaze with fresh swamp greens salad). Then I excused myself—said I needed to study for the Monster Achievement Test and practice Scare

Patrol tactics. I was kind of surprised when my dad offered to help.

Pap threw his bulky arm around my shoulders. "That's my monster," he said.

I blinked. When was the last time he'd said that?

"Mondo! Mon-dOOOOOO!" Mam shrieked as she floated into the dining room. "Ghoulbert's done it again. My bungling big boy. My misaligned monster."

"What now?" Pap hunched his shoulders, as though preparing for a blow.

"Ghoulbert's gotten his head stuck in the toilet again. Trying to rescue Spidey."

"Ratzbotchin!" Pap threw back his thick green noggin. "That silly pet spider causing trouble again, Shareeka? Hiding out to get another bite on my behind, I bet. I've a mind to flatten that spider. Flatter than a nail in a coffin."

"Oh, drat, draaaaaat, draaaaaat," wailed Mam. "You mustn't." She floated on Pap's footsteps, as he stomped to the outhouse.

I slipped quietly away. I knew by the time this latest crisis was solved Pap would be ready for his pre-bedtime nap by the fireplace. All I needed to do was leave a note on my now carefully rumpled bed, "Went for a midnight stroll," in case someone tried to look in on me.

A SHORT WHILE later, I stood camouflaged in the cemetery shadows, waiting for Georgina. Weepy clouds, like half-closed eyelids, shrouded the tops of the two moons. The quartered gray spots peeked from beneath the clouds. They seemed to spy down on me with cold intensity. I slid behind an ancient skeleton tree, taking shelter from the moons' glare. As I pressed my neck against the cool, smooth tree bark, I shivered. And not in a good way.

Never had I felt so unwelcome in the cemetery before. I guessed it must be like what humans experience when they step through such rusted, creeper covered gates—fearful of each shadow, jumping with each sound. Rather than what a monster—a rightful heir to all the wonder entombed within this hallowed sight—should feel. It was as though the ground that I walked on knew my unmonsterly intentions. As if it readied to throw me out, for I didn't belong, didn't deserve to be here.

With a sweaty palm I tugged on my backpack, slung over one shoulder. It held all the needed spell ingredients. My brain stored the recipe directions to share with Zelda. Witches seldom shared secret recipes—especially Granny Bubbie who had been something of a conjuring mastermind. She'd always hoarded her spell collection with zest.

I traced the now almost invisible X on my palm. But Granny Bubbie had shared this recipe all right—most forcefully. It certainly seemed that she was leading me down an awfully dangerous path. Just when I was trying my best to fit in.

Ghostbumps sprouted above the X and raced up my arm. I slapped my tingling hand against the tree's smooth, hard bark. Granny Bubbie couldn't want me exiled—or worse. I moaned when I considered that hurtful thought. No. Granny Bubbie had always been the one who understood me.

"Ratzbotchin!" I muttered, echoing Pap's earlier curse. My heart thump-bumped in my chest. I knew Granny Bubbie's plans for me would be meant for the best. Still, it seemed, especially toward the end of her ancient witchy days, that her plans had too often gone awry.

When I heard the flurry of wings above me in the cemetery, I stepped out of the shadow into the misty moonlight. Georgina executed a soft landing nearby.

"Here," I called. My voice was little more than a whisper. I waved my right hand. The tingle still tickled my palm.

FROM the GRAVE

Behind me, the snap of a broken skeleton tree twig echoed in the midnight silence. I spun around.

A voice called from the shadows. "Frank?"

A familiar shape glowed. Loose linen strips reflected the moonlight. "Oliver! What are you doing here?"

"You two need help."

Georgina gurgled. "He's right. We might."

I shook my head so hard my neck bolts rattled. "No! No! And NO!"

Oliver held out a mostly unwrapped hand. "Misfit teamwork. Isn't that what you said? To show we are monster enough."

"This is too dangerous. Especially for you."

"You can't stop me." Oliver edged close to Georgina.

"Come on," she said. "We need to go!"

"No. None of us are going." Surprisingly my words sounded calm. I stepped between Oliver and Georgina. "This was a crazy plan from the start. Georgina may know how to take care of herself, but I won't let my best friend be annihilated in some stupid stunt to prove we're monsters."

Oliver drew a finger to his lips, his eyes wide.

A loosened rock crunched behind a jangleberry bush close by, followed by a muttered curse.

Another monster stalked us.

"Do you see something?" I whispered, yanking Oliver close.

Georgina shook her head.

I motioned for them both to follow. We three huddled behind the large dragon mausoleum near the gate.

A bat squeaked and a familiar voice rose among the gravestones.

"Blasted boogers!" It was Malcolm. I edged closer.

A throaty voice demanded, "Come out from there."

I sucked in a breath. It was Ms. Hagmire. I peered around

the crypt. There she stood with her claws on her hips, wrapped in a hooded cloak and trailing a long scarf.

"Now!" she commanded.

Malcolm slunk into the open.

"Were you spying on me?" she asked.

He shook his head. His hair tuft bobbed when he answered. "No. I swear."

"Hummmmpf. Who were you spying on then?"

"No one," he said, digging a hoof into the crumbly soil. But I knew who he'd been after. I sucked in another deep breath. If Malcolm ratted on us, our rescue attempt would end right here.

"Now you're choosing to lie," said Ms. Hagmire with a toss of her head. "Which is your prerogative. But I've no time for troll tales tonight. I'm sure you are up to no good, as you should be."

She reached out with a long, grimy claw, twisting the cord around Malcolm's neck. Tight, tight, tighter! He grunted. With a final jerk, she flipped the shark tooth up, clipping his warty nose. Malcolm snorted from the sting, but he remained frozen under her paralyzing stare.

"I'm warning you, McNastee. Whatever you are up to had better not concern me. Not me or any of my students." She paused, looking quickly to where we hid. Her words were spoken louder than before. "It's my business to help them . . . be monster enough! Do you understand?"

He pulled his head back and drew away, still holding tight to the shark tooth.

Ms. Hagmire rewound the knotted scarf about her long neck. Again she threw a glance in our direction then slyly dropped something onto the moonlit path behind her. I stared in disbelief. My eyes must be playing tricks on me in the evening gloom.

Our teacher's voice took my attention back to her and Malcolm. "Enjoy your midnight stroll, McNastee. But beware. Frightful creatures lurk ever so close. Creatures that can't wait for you to take a tumble—if The Rules are disregarded." Once again she looked our way. "Do remember the Demon Hours."

Malcolm gave another clumsy snort. He and our teacher quickly faded into the cemetery wonders, walking away in opposite directions.

"Hurry," said Georgina. "Let's go!"

"I'll be right back." With long steps, I scampered to the trail. There it was—my forbidden comb!

I ran my fingers over it—feeling only slight damage from piranha nibbles. With a quick swipe, I ran it through my tousled hair, sighing as the tangles smoothed. Suddenly I felt like myself again. Sure and confident.

How had Ms. Hagmire found my comb? And why had she dropped it here? I shoved it deep into my pocket. She'd told Malcolm, "It's my business to help them be monster enough." Her covert message sent my neck bolts thrumming. She couldn't have any idea we were returning to Exxillium, could she? I took a deep breath. It didn't matter if she knew or not because now I knew.

We were monster enough to rescue Zelda and Mr. McNastee.

Quickly and quietly, I slunk back to Georgina's side. Oliver already sat atop her back.

I opened my mouth but before I could speak, Georgina silenced me. "No time to argue." Her wings started flapping. "Monster or die," she said.

I shook my head but climbed up, holding tight behind my best friend.

Through the growing mist, we ascended as silently as possible. With my friends around me, my comb in my pocket, and maybe my teacher's consent, I was setting out on the adventure of a lifetime. I grinned. "Monster on!"

CHAPTER NINETEEN

Monster Rule #85: Monsters must find a way to monster, no matter the circumstances.

FRANK'S TALE

Georgina proved to be a more stable aircraft than Witch Picklepuss and her notorious broom. With less stomach pains to contend with, I had plenty of time to fill Oliver in on our plans.

"So we'll land on the far side of the island?"

"Yep, that's what Mr. McNastee suggested last night," Georgina said.

"Hopefully the Minotaurs aren't patrolling there," said Oliver with a shiver.

Georgina gurgled. "They saw me when I was leaving last night, and I had to make up a real warttoad of a lie. Said I was trying to fly to the Badlands Quagmire to see the young swamp monster races, but I wasn't too good at directions and lost my way."

"They believed you?" Oliver asked.

"I guess they figured my flying was as mixed up as my dragon breath. Plus, I think their horns are much sharper than their brains. When they started snorting and saying that the races weren't held in Shocktober but only in months starting with *R*, I told them the new rule was months ending with *R*."

"Quick thinking, Georgina." I snickered. All Uggarland months ended in *R*.

"Well, it distracted 'em long enough for me to make my exit. Plus, they probably figured I'd never find my way back to Uggarland. Me being such a misfit."

I took a deep breath. "If we do run into the Minotaurs, I've got a . . . uh . . . special weapon." At least I hoped. "But best if we can avoid them."

"For sure," agreed Oliver.

My stomach fluttered. A match-up with the Minotaurs would totally test my new firepower. A candle flame wouldn't hold off two angry Minotaurs. I sincerely hoped I could generate a bigger blaze than that. If only Granny had given me a little more time to perfect my skill before testing it in battle.

"I've set up rooms for Zelda and Mr. McNastee at Granny's house," I said, holding tight as Georgina started her descent. "No one will look there for the time being. And I did some research in Granny's spell book for disguises. They might need to transform temporarily to avoid being caught once we get back." I was careful not to say, "IF we get back."

"Good idea," said Georgina.

Oliver leaned forward as we descended. His words were almost snatched up by the wind and the surf pounding against the shore. "Sounds like a pretty good plan actually."

I shook my wind-blown head, fearing there was something I'd forgotten in this impromptu plan. But if so, it was too late now. Georgina glided to a soft landing on the far side beach.

Mr. McNastee and Zelda emerged from beneath a rocky overhang. This side of the island had more rocks than beach. I stumbled as I attempted to tiptoe among the scattered stones. Frankensteins don't tiptoe easily.

"Frank!" Malcolm's dad stepped from the shadows and patted me on the back. "I'm very glad to see you again." Zelda edged beside him, gripping her hat in her hands. She nodded a silent "hello."

"Remember Oliver?" I asked.

"I remember you," said Zelda. "Three's kind of a crowd though."

"Wasn't my idea," I said shrugging, "but he wanted to help."

"More's the scarier!" said Mr. McNasee thumping Oliver on the back.

"We need to hurry." Georgina's clipped words held a hint of fear. "I spotted some banks of clouds forming on the flight over. If it starts storming, it'll be hard for me to carry both Frank and Mr. McNastee—and maybe even Oliver, if Zelda can't handle a rider." She clenched and re-clenched her small claws. "The three of us . . . we have a lot to lose if this doesn't work."

"We all do," said Mr. McNastee. "And we greatly appreciate your valiant efforts. All of you. In my Scare Patrol missions, I'm sure I've never been with braver monsters than you three."

My stomach fluttered. But not from the flight. I didn't feel brave at all. With each step on the sandy shore, I felt the exact opposite of monsterly. A monster wouldn't be helping outcasts escape Exxillium. No matter what Granny Bubbie had said about not following the pack, this plan seemed downright stupid. With that thought, a zap of pain shot through my right hand. Turning up my palm, I saw the green *X* glowing bright.

"Okay, I get it! I get it!" I muttered beneath my breath. My departed granny still urged me on. I slipped my comb from my pocket and smoothed down my windblown hair. Ah, that felt better.

I pulled off my backpack. My fingers fumbled as I tried to

retrieve the two toadstool gills, five dizzy bug eyelids, and three knuckles worth of dingdang dung.

"Ah." Mr. McNastee inhaled. "It smells like home already."

With a glance at Zelda, my bolts zinged. Something was missing! "Where's your broom?" I asked, nearly choking on my words.

"What?" Zelda's voice was ice.

"Your broom," I said. "The spell is supposed to cure you of your fear of flying. Witches can't fly without their brooms."

"I don't have a broom," gasped Zelda. "I never earned one. I thought you meant to cure me of my fear of heights. I thought Georgina would fly us all back."

"Snotfargle!" I kicked my foot into the sand.

"Sorry," said Georgina. "I guess I didn't explain things so well."

"Ooze buckets! It's my fault for not planning this good enough on such short notice." I motioned to the sky. "Look! There are hardly any stars showing through now." I raised my nose and sniffed. A storm was certainly brewing. "We three better scary back to Uggarland before it's too late. Sorry, but we've got to scratch this rescue."

"No! Wait." Roary McNastee grabbed my arm when I started to stuff the ingredients into my backpack. "Don't leave us. Please. We . . . we just need to find something that will work."

"What about that shovel Zelda had yesterday?" said Oliver.

My hand glowed hotter. "Well, I guess it does have a handle like a broom. That's at least half right."

"Would that work, Zelda?" Georgina asked.

"Sure. Okay. I mean, can't we try it? Please." Zelda reached for the backpack. Her cold, shaking hands clamped over mine. The X pulsed in my palm. Zelda froze. I knew she felt it, too. Her hands stilled. The warmth spread into Zelda's fingers. She sighed—as though she'd spotted an old friend.

"Booger bandits!" I pulled my hands from Zelda's. "Okay, okay. But how are we going to get it? We're trying not to be noticed. Remember?"

Zelda flapped her hat against her side. "The shovel's in the garden on top of the hill. At least, it's not all the way back in the village."

"Lucky us," I said, cringing as a gust of rain-scented wind messed up my hair. Georgina gurgled. Mr. McNastee tugged on his droopy ear, looking even more bent over. A rumble of distant thunder echoed above, as Oliver quickly pulled more and more strips away. The parts of his unwrapped nut-brown body almost disappeared into the dark night.

"We need to hurry, Frank," said Georgina again.

I threw back my Frankenstein head and moaned. Scare or be scared. Thunder rumbled closer. Scare . . . scared . . . Scare Patrol!

"That's it!" I said, grabbing one of Oliver's last loose ends and pulling it off. Oliver stood in his linen undershorts, almost invisible. "We'll use a monster Scare Patrol alternative strategy. Divide and regroup." I began diagramming the plan with my big blue hands. "Georgina, you fly Oliver back to the garden. He'll sneak in and get the shovel. I'll help Zelda with the potion, so by the time you come back we'll be ready. Mr. McNastee will keep a look out."

"Excellent plan," said Malcolm's dad.

"You okay with that Oliver?" I asked. It wasn't easy to see if my nearly invisible friend was shaking or not.

"I'm okay," said Oliver, lightly punching my arm.

I nodded.

Oliver, freed from his wrappings, took three long strides then vaulted onto Georgina's back like a gremlin pretending to be a circus acrobat at the Halloween Feast.

"Wow," said Zelda. "I didn't know a mummy could do that."

"He's not just any mummy," I said grinning, so happy to see the old, acrobatic Oliver back. "He's my best friend."

"But you've got to hurry," I said. "And, ah, don't get caught again, Georgina. Even those goofy Minotaurs won't believe any more of your lies."

Georgina flicked me with her tail. "We got it. We're all scared. We'll do our best."

"Our best," I echoed, turning to Zelda. "You do know how to mix up potions, don't you?"

Zelda grabbed the dingdang dung from the backpack. "Of course, I do. I'm not the total drizzlepoop you think I am." She paused. "It's only flying I have a problem with and heights—and a bit of farsightedness."

Georgina gurgled. "And we have one more problem. A raindrop just fell!"

"Monster madness!" I muttered. I thrust my hands into my backpack. "Here," I cried, shoving a pair of Granny's old goggles into Zelda's hands. "I threw these in when I was loading up the potion ingredients. My hand wouldn't stop stinging until I did. Guess I know why now."

Malcolm's dad squeezed Zelda in a hefty troll hug. "They'll work. I'm sure they'll work, Zelda. You mix up the potion with Frank. I'll keep watch and those two will be back with the shovel faster than a glowworm's flash."

The first streak of lightning lit the sky as Georgina and Oliver rose into it.

Huh! I gasped. Had I seen a pair of monster eyes spying on us from beneath the rocky outcrop? My neck bolts zinged!

CHAPTER TWENTY

*Monster Rule #41: A monster's growl, no matter how horrific,
is never worse than its bite. Beware!*

MALCOLM'S TALE

Ms. Hagmire had slunk away into the blackness, leaving me alone in the cemetery silence. Just the way I liked it. I climbed to the top of the Ancients Mound and surveyed the gloom. No sign of Frank. I must make this problem become an opportunity. Monster it for all its potential. I would wait. And watch. I would sink into the stillness. Become one with the darkness. I would tune into my enemy's energy—his essence. I would find him.

The drear deepened. The mist stalked higher. I stretched my cramped legs. I shook the cobwebs from my head and tried to stay alert. My watch continued.

I knew exactly what was expected of a monster. I might not be the best at Math or History or, especially, UnSocial Studies. I couldn't remember when the first Hydra serpent's head had been cut off and two more sprouted in its place. Nor could I easily create a Minotaur's labyrinth.

FROM the GRAVE

Although tonight had gone exceptionally wrong, I generally excelled at Scare Tactics—Growling, Frightening, and Sneakiness. I could track my prey on silent hooves for hours. I could form the most sinister, slow-growing, deep, raspy growl. It vibrated from the base of my throat. It rose up into my wide-open jaw like a winged creature, doubling in volume as it echoed in my mouth. The growl would pounce on my victim, who by then would be shaking with terror.

My gruesome growl that I'd learned from my father.

What would he think of me now? I snorted. Who cared what the outcast would think. The mutant. The misfit. I hated him, of course. As I should. As I must.

The thoughts in my head kept twisting and turning, like the snakes atop a Medusa's head. Still I wondered what it would feel like to have him hug me tight just one more time.

"Pus nuggets!" Too much thinking and not enough monstering. I'd get myself in trouble if I let these crazy thoughts slither about in my brain. I must rely on my monster instincts. I knew good from bad better than most monsters. My father was bad. He was a loser. Period. An outcast on Exxillium. Soon to implode or dry up and be gone. End of the nightmare.

No other monsters were going to find out about him. About Roary McNastee. About his horrific stain on our family honor. Poor Grandma Ooogle would have leaped into the shredder if she'd known of my father's waywardness. I pressed the shark tooth she'd given me against my chest but found little comfort in its familiar feel.

And Frank. That freakish odd bat. Somehow always meddling in my life. First, teaching Nelly tidy ways. Now, finding out the family secret; discovering it before I even knew.

I snarled. Where had Frankenstein Gordon disappeared to on this Tooshday night? He was up to evil, of that I was sure.

I snarled louder. One way or the other, Frank would have to forget he'd ever heard of my father. I held a clenched claw up to the overcast sky. I vowed to make very, very sure of that.

CHAPTER TWENTY-ONE

Monster Rule #139: Monster might is multiplied through collaboration.

FRANK'S TALE

With surprising speed and skill, Zelda poured and stirred. She mixed the ingredients in the small bowl I'd borrowed from Granny Bubbie's cupboard. Granny's spell book was such a jumble and her writing such scritch-scratching. I sure hoped I'd deciphered it correctly.

Under her breath, Zelda repeated the spell as I taught it to her. But could a witch who couldn't even fly, truly know how to do a spell? Perhaps I was misjudging her as much as the others misjudged us O.M.O students. Thunder rumbled ever closer.

"I've got it," she said after the third attempt.

"What we don't have is the shovel. And we aren't even sure it will work as a broom." I scanned the dark horizon. "Scumtwattle! Where are they?"

Zelda spoke with a strange authority. "They're on their way back with the shovel."

"How do you know?"

She shrugged. "I can't read minds or a crystal ball like most

witches, but sometimes I can see . . . see what's happening somewhere else. And I, um, I see at least one of the Minotaurs headed
to this side of the island."

I gulped. "A . . . Minotaur. Are you sure?"

She nodded, her hat flopping crazily atop her head. "But
not here yet."

A flash of lightning illuminated the beach, brighter than
even the most gloomless monster midday. I twirled around. I'd
seen something move near the rock overhang where Zelda and
Mr. McNastee had been hiding. I grabbed Zelda's arm, nearly
overturning the potion.

"Watch out!" she cried.

"Look. Over there." I pointed. "Did you see something?"

"No. I was concentrating on the spell."

Mr. McNastee strolled down the dark beach in the other
direction. If I called out to him, I might alert whatever watched
from beneath the rocks. I peered toward the outcrop. I sensed
something there. Why couldn't Zelda's supposed "seeing" powers see what it was?

"I'm going to check it out."

"Wait." Her voice pulled me back. "What if it's an injured sea
monster, or what if I'm wrong? And it is the other Minotaur.
You can't fight off their attack alone."

I gulped. "But what if it's not a sea monster or a Minotaur
hiding there?"

"I don't understand."

"What if it's one of the outcasts and not a monster? What
if you two were followed?"

"We were careful," Zelda insisted. "No one saw us leave.
The sun makes everyone so tired here. It's almost impossible
to stay awake to enjoy the night. I'm sure. No one saw us. But
if there is someone spying, I . . . I can cast a forgetful spell on
them. It's super easy. They won't remember a thing."

No matter how positive her words, Zelda's voice held a hint of doubt.

I grabbed a large piece of driftwood and held it aloft in my left hand. With a few large Frankenstein steps, I was halfway to the overhang before my thoughts caught up to my actions. My knees shook beneath me. I took a deep breath. I smelled fear but couldn't be sure if it was mine or another's.

Something waited for me in the darkness ahead. A creature trembling or licking its chops. A streak of lightning illuminated the beach. The driftwood quivered in my hand. There. In the sand. A trail. Without a doubt, something or someone was under the overhang.

Holding my right palm over the driftwood, I willed the heat into my hand. With a zap, a flame shot out from the X. The dry wood caught fire.

"Leaping lizards! It worked!" I held it before me like a torch. Taking a shaky step forward, I bent under the overhang. The cavernous place was filled with dark corners and openings back into the hillside. A trail in the sand led to one of the crevices. Bending lower, I started to push the torch toward the black hole.

But suddenly a soft flutter above stopped me. I looked back over my shoulder to see Georgina and Oliver dropping almost silently to the beach. Mr. McNastee trotted toward us.

"Frank," Zelda hissed. She motioned me back. "Frank!"

The torchlight fire crackled in my ear. I eyed the shadowed opening. Nothing moved.

"Put out that fire," Zelda called, "or someone might see us."

I dropped the driftwood, extinguishing the flame in the sand, and quickly retraced my steps. But I felt a set of eyes follow my return.

"Here," said Oliver gasping. He held out the shovel.

Zelda clasped the scraggly shovel to her chest. A lightning bolt split the sky. In a blink, thunder boomed. Salty spray hit my face. The amped-up winds tugged at my tattered clothes. The storm was almost on top of us.

Georgina panted as well. "The Minotaurs. They . . . saw us!"

"And they're coming," said Oliver.

"Do it! The spell." Georgina cried. "Now!"

"Sure." Zelda's voice didn't sound sure though. Her hands shook as she placed the goggles over her eyes. Mr. McNastee helped steady her as she drew the bowl to her lips.

"Wait!" My stinging right hand yanked the bowl away. A dollop of the potion splashed on my fingers. "The spell. You have to say it before you drink it."

"Oh, yeah. Of course." Zelda's eyes—behind the thick goggles—opened wide. She spread her hands over the potion as a raindrop hit my nose. "Help me," she cried to all three of us. "Don't let any water into the bowl. It could contaminate the potion. And poison me."

Georgina spread her wings over Zelda. Mr. McNastee and I crowded around the young witch. My right hand sizzled as the raindrops hit. Fresh pain pulsed through the scar and threatened to upend me. Wasn't this rescue what Granny Bubbie had wanted me to do? Help Zelda fly. I gulped. Perhaps I had totally misread the signs.

Another blaze of lightning. It bounced off the cliff nearby. Sparks flashed around us. Was that a Minotaur roar rumbling with the thunder?

"Now! Now!" Georgina said.

A jolt of pain tore through my hand as though the lightning had struck me with a direct hit. My hand flapped of its own accord and tangled itself in Zelda's long black hair. My thumb and forefinger pinched together. My hand jerked back.

"Bunion pus!" Zelda cried out in pain. "You've ripped a chunk of my hair out."

FROM the GRAVE

My hand hovered over the potion bowl and dropped the hair into it.

"Um," I mumbled, "I forgot to mention the last ingredient. A lock of your hair." Only a tingle now pulsed into my fingertips.

Zelda's green eyes flashed. "And you couldn't have just asked?"

"He forgot to bring scissors, I'm guessing," said Oliver.

I shrugged my Frankenstein shoulders. "Sorry."

"No worries," said Mr. McNastee. "Onward and inward. Drink up."

Zelda stirred the potion with a long fingernail. She bent low over the bowl and recited the rehearsed words aloud.

"Fears of flying,
Flying fears.
Witch's worries,
Witch's tears.
Now all mended—
Fortified.
Now transformed—
Fly the sky!"

A sky full of zigzagged lightning bolts broke the night into craggy pieces. Zelda gulped down the frothing potion as icy pellets of rain beat upon our hunched backs.

She sneezed. A puff of smoke shot from her nostrils. I handed her the shovel. Zelda's magnified eyes peered through the ungainly goggles. Her eyes seemed wildly out of focus, but she swung her right leg over the shovel without a mishap.

Like a monster tot who's discovered a hidden nest of newt eggs in her breakfast gruel, Zelda's mouth opened in surprise. Her feet no longer touched the gritty sand.

"The shovel works!" I cried.

To celebrate, Oliver did an amazing cartwheel in the sand.

"Monster mind over matter," said Georgina, clapping.

Zelda looped a low circle around us. Then she rose higher, skidding to a stop in mid-air. A wide-eyed young witch looked down at us. The misfit seemed to have disappeared.

"I'm not scared! Not at all!"

"Magic never ceases to amaze, does it? Even for an old monster like me." Malcolm's dad raised his head to the pelting rain, defying its threat to steal his essence. A low, powerful growl erupted from his open jaws.

I too tossed back my head and let the raindrops bombard me. I knew now that no water could wash away my monster essence. We all had plenty to spare. Each of us was more than monster enough. I howled with the joy of it.

"We'll celebrate when we get back," cried Georgina above the storm's din. "Hurry! Or we won't make it before the Demon Hours."

"Or before the Minotaurs," said Zelda.

The storm seemed to pause for a moment as Georgina motioned for us to climb on. Only a few sprinkles fell when Oliver grabbed his pile of discarded wrappings. I slung my backpack onto my shoulders. With an effortless leap, Oliver took his place on Georgina's back.

It was then that the shouts rang out.

"Halt!" The larger Minotaur galloped from behind the rocky outcrop. With a roar, the second beast charged toward us, both swinging their broadaxes through the air.

"What the hailstone!" Mr. McNastee cursed. With a hefty shoulder thrust, I pushed him up behind Oliver. Georgina already hovered off the ground.

"Get on, Frank!" Zelda cried, floating beside me. Before I could even consider if first time flyer Zelda could manage a passenger, I threw a leg over the shovel. My behind rested on the flattened blade.

FROM the GRAVE

The Minotaurs thundered toward us, eyes glowing red in the black of night.

"Take it up, Zelda! Higher!" I boomed.

"I'm trying!" Still, we hovered only a few feet off the ground. Georgina and her two passengers had already climbed above our heads.

Whoosh! An axe sliced off the sole of my boot, nicking my blue foot. I grimaced. A Minotaur claw grabbed my left ankle. Another pulled on my right leg. I kicked hard, nearly falling from the shovel.

"Whoa!" Zelda cried. "I'm tipping over!"

Georgina dive-bombed the Minotaurs, gushing a huge spray of water right into their faces. They snorted and shook their heads. With that momentary distraction, Oliver did an acrobatic leap from Georgina, landing near the farthest Minotaur. Oliver clutched one of his long mummy strips. With a whirl of fancy footwork, Oliver wrapped the strip around the creature's legs. Mr. McNastee, holding the other end, yanked on the strip.

"Oooof!" sputtered the Minotaur. He tripped and tumbled into the other brute. With a final kick, I pulled free and pushed the guards away.

"Rooooaaaaarrr!" thundered the guards, scrambling for their dropped axes.

"Watch out!" I cried. Oliver backflipped to avoid a blow. Georgina swung around to retrieve him. I held out my right hand, aiming a fiery blast.

Zzzzt! Nothing! Not even a spark. "Rat splat!" I cried in frustration and warning.

With no time to spare, Oliver somersaulted through Goon One's legs and raced to Georgina's side. He grabbed Mr. McNastee's extended arm and sprung aboard.

"Wow!" said Georgina. "You sure didn't learn those mummy moves at school."

"That's for sure," I muttered, still upset that my magic hadn't worked to protect my friend. Was Granny's magic all gone?

Georgina zoomed past the Minotaurs, whirling sand and spray in her wake. The two raging bulls fell back further, shielding their heads with their muscled arms. They snorted, sinking to the sand. Another lightning strike was followed by an immediate thunder clap. The rain came back with a fury.

"Let's monster out of here—now!" I yelled my plea into Zelda's hat, hoping she had figured out how to maneuver with a passenger. We still hovered much too low.

"I've got one more thing to throw at them before we leave," called out Zelda. She muttered a quick verse and spat in the Minotaurs direction. "Don't want them to remember what happened. They'd report you for sure."

"Will that spell really work?"

"For a while at least, I hope."

I gulped. Another part of the plan I'd not accounted for. We should have borrowed some of Nelly's Halloween gear, although it's not easy to camouflage dragons or Frankensteins.

As the shovel sputtered, I tried to shoot off one last fire blast. All I could manage was a smoky 'poof!' Zelda, too, was having trouble managing her new magic. First we veered back inland, wobbling almost uncontrollably. A blade sliced through the air, clanging against the shovel.

"Oooof!" cried Zelda, fighting to regain control. The shovel handle plunged down. The sand rose up. The rocks seemed to zoom straight in our path.

"Take us up!" I yelled.

With both hands, Zelda yanked on the shovel handle. We zipped upward, but not before my bucket-size Frankenstein feet clipped a hillside rock. More gashes!

"Beezle bung!" I yelled, smarting from the impact. Finally, Zelda righted the shovel and we slowly climbed aloft, lifting out of the Minotaurs' reach. They shook their claws at us, yelling monster curses, until the misty clouds swallowed us up.

Georgina drew close. "We'll fly as low as we can," she called to us.

"Hey! No way," Zelda said. "I want to see how high this shovel will soar."

"Huh? I didn't sign on for any aerodynamics with a driver-in-training," I said with a gulp.

"I'm not being cautious because this is your maiden flight," said Georgina, over the rumbling storm. "It's because the winds will be higher aloft. Neither of us can afford to get blown off our flight plan. A straight line is the shortest route, especially when we're both carrying cargo." Georgina yelled the final words as she shot ahead. "Stay close to my tail."

"Oh, all right," grumbled Zelda. But as the last glimpse of Exxillium peeked through the clouds, the new teen pilot yelled a resounding "Woooo—hoooo!!!"

Holding tight, I couldn't help but smile. Zelda's triumphant yell made my neck bolts tingle.

CHAPTER TWENTY-TWO

Monster Rule #65: An alert monster is an alive monster.

MALCOLM'S TALE

When I finally stood to stretch my cramped legs, a sharp stone wedged into my hoof. "Snotfargle!" I exhaled a mouthful of curses into the chilled cemetery damp. I snorted and tried to dig out the embedded stone.

I'd lost Frank's trail. I'd wasted a midnight ramble. And now an icy pain shot up my leg from waiting so long on misfits. I'd been out-monstered by Frank—and that interfering Ms. Hagmire. I refused to be out-monstered.

With a "Grrrrooooowlllll!" I finally managed to pop the stone from my hoof. My cry bounced off the tombstones but offered little comfort. Snatching up the stone, I hurled it against the brittle skeleton tree blocking my view of the half moons. My expedition. It was too late. Too poorly executed. Somehow gone wrong.

A night vulture screeched above.

I perked up my ears. The Last Bells would soon toll out the end for monster walkabouts. My tail twitched when I re-membered how quickly the Demon Hours had descended on me last night. I would not dare the evil time two nights in a row—especially when my monster powers seemed to ebb so low.

With a disgruntled huff, I slip-slid down the slick slope. My hooves dug rough grooves in the packed dirt. I skidded to the bottom, righted myself, and trotted through the cemetery gates. I slammed the iron bars shut behind me. Their clang echoed in my ears as I rounded the corner and headed for home. The lone howl of a distant werewolf carried through the mist. But as I angled past the last bit of marshy ground surrounding the apartment's fence, my head snapped up.

A boom. A screech. A squeal.

Before I realized it, I trotted toward the sounds. I braked to a stop amid the rough bladed swamp grass.

My nose and my ears pulled me beyond the apartment complex—down a nearly deserted adjacent street. Mushington Way.

The street had only three witches' houses on it. I knew the first one belonged to Ghoulbert's grandma. No one had lived in it since her accident years ago, but often Frank visited it. I snorted. Even the threat of the Demon Hours wouldn't stop me from seeking out my enemy one last time this night. With stealthy steps, I quickly made my way to the house.

My tail switched back and forth. I sniff, sniff, sniffed. Then I smiled.

Yes, I was sure. A hint of clean. A wisp of Gurglenut Chewies. It was Frank. Very near.

He would not escape me this time. I slid into the bushes.

But then, a growl chilled me to the bone. A growl so familiar—never to be forgotten. I peeked through the jangleberry bush.

Without a doubt I knew who it was. My father. Standing there.

But how? He was an exile. On Exxillium. Somehow he had escaped! I crouched deeper behind the bush. Frank, picking up a hat, had nearly stumbled upon me. The stupid pus nugget!

But as hard as I tried, I couldn't stop my panting. The too-loud pounding of my heart in my orange chest.

A fuzzy buzzing filled my ears. My head teetered on my short neck.

My father. My father.

I tried to take a breath. My lips formed into a snarl. I bit it back.

Roary McNastee. My *misfit* father. Here now for all Monster City to see. An odd monster out. And I feared to think what that made me.

CHAPTER TWENTY-THREE

Monster Rule #53: Nightmares do come true.

FRANK'S TALE

With a low growl, Mr. McNastee righted himself.

I pulled myself up from the ground. I'd tumbled there when Zelda smashed the two of us into the cellar door. Mr. McNastee had been holding it open for Georgina. Oliver had stood nearby, rewrapping a few strips.

When Zelda and I'd fallen, so had the cellar door. It smashed down on Georgina's head then pinched her tail. She'd let out a yelp loud enough to wake even the drowsiest zombie. And from the sound of it, she'd fallen down the stairs—almost taking Mr. McNastee with her.

I yanked Zelda to her feet. "Ouch!" she cried, grabbing her foot.

"What were you doing? Did your goggles fog up?" My head bubbled with anger and fatigue—and a new bump. "Georgina told you to slow down for the landing."

"I know. I know." Limping, Zelda pushed her goggles to her forehead. "Hey, where's my hat?" She patted the dark ground, feeling for her toppled hat. "I wanted to try a swoop around the trees. Guess I got a little dizzy. Like you wouldn't have gone for it on your first flight."

"No, I would not! Not carrying a passenger and not when you were supposed to fly as quietly as possible!"

"Oh, kind of like how you're practically yelling now!"

Mr. McNastee poked his snout between us. "Crusted creeps! You two need to keep it down. Georgina's taken quite a tumble. Are you all right?"

"I've twisted my ankle." Zelda answered before I could. She still searched for her missing hat. "But I'll survive."

"So happy to hear that," I muttered.

Mr. McNastee trotted back down to check on Georgina.

"Give it a rest," said Zelda. "We made it, didn't we? Help me find my hat."

"I'll help," said Oliver, stepping between us. He was more unwrapped than wrapped.

"Hey," said Mr. McNastee, peeking out of the cellar. "We've got trouble."

Just as I grabbed Zelda's lost hat from beneath a jangleberry bush, Georgina's droopy head rose from the cellar. "I'm . . . ah, not doing too well." She stumbled out. Stirring up a small cloud of dust, she plopped onto the ground.

"Don't lay down!" I cried. "We have to leave now. We can't be out during the Demon Hours! That will be worse than the Minotaurs."

Without even thinking, I twisted Zelda's hat in my hands. I didn't want to imagine the consequences. We couldn't be out when all evil was free to roam in Uggarland. Ms. Hagmire had told us only those with true evil in their hearts dared be afoot in the Demon Hours.

Georgina managed to push herself up. Her head still wobbled though.

FROM the GRAVE

"Can you fly?" I asked. "Just to your house?"

"Maybe." Georgina took a deep breath and weakly fluttered her wings.

"Aaaargh!" The cry exploded from my throat. The heat boiled in me. I should have had a backup plan for this too.

Or a better first plan: Do NOT rescue misfits from Exxillium.

I doubled up my fist and punched it through Zelda's hat. The material ripped easily.

"What did you do?" Zelda grabbed her battered hat and pushed me away. "What if I can't fix it? A witch can't witch without a hat." Zelda's eyes blazed. "Find your own way home. We'll take care of Georgina here tonight."

Oliver nudged me. I looked into his wide-open eyes then dropped my head, too embarrassed to say anything. I took three quick breaths of the damp, swamp-soaked air. At least this time, my anger evaporated as quickly as it had come. Still, I couldn't look at Zelda as I spoke. "Sorry," I said.

Zelda's voice was scratchy; barely a whisper, but I heard it loud and clear. "Thank you."

"Sure," I mumbled, watching Zelda slowly descend the cellar stairs. She favored her hurt foot. A misty batch of night fog rolled about us. "Come on, Oliver. We gotta hurry." I managed to flash a low flame from my palm toward the path ahead. At least a bit of Granny's magic still seemed to be there.

"You've got some new tricks tonight too," he said, pointing to the flame.

"Yeah, too little too late though."

But as we readied to trot away, the magic seemed to flare up. Although the flame sputtered and died, my right hand burned. The magic was alerting me to danger. Before I could call out in alarm, my hand clamped tight over my mouth.

I motioned for the others to be silent. I tried to zero in

on each night sound around me. The wind's howl down the darkened street. A night vulture's flapping wings overhead. And . . . over there. The raspy panting of something hidden in the bushes opposite the cellar door.

A monster watched us!

CHAPTER TWENTY-FOUR

Monster Rule #333: Evil is mayhem orchestrated for untoward purposes.

MALCOLM'S TALE

I tried to still my breathing. My heart raced. Snotfargle! Had they seen me?

Frank whispered something to the mummy.

Even my misfit father was on alert. He signaled to the others. Georgina snuffled and flapped her wings. She whispered a few words down the steps to that teen witch then dropped the cellar door in place. Next she nodded to my father. With a short sniff, he sprinted forward, right toward my hiding spot.

With a growl, I leaped from the bush and sprinted across the road toward home. I had to make it. Before they caught me. Before the Last Bells.

"Catch him!" he called.

My mutant father's strides were fast. Frank, and that mummy too, raced across Mushington Way behind him. The dragon flew above, cutting off a direct path to my apartment. Instead, I veered into the thick swamp grasses behind the complex, hoping to lose them.

I huffed. They were gaining ground. I plowed into the tall grass near the swamp water's edge.

"Arrrrghhh!" My father's growl reached my ears before his claws pulled me down. "I've got him."

We snorted and scuffled. My nostrils soaked up his once familiar scent. My body went limp. His strong claws held me firm.

Frank and the mummy huffed to a stop. "Malcolm!" Frank cried.

"Malcolm?" my father echoed. But anything else he might have been about to say was stopped by the gong.

BAAAAROOOOONGGG!!!

BAAAAROOOOONGGG!!!

The Last Bells! The dreaded gong blasted against our ears. I quivered. The evil ones were about to descend!

"Oh no!" screamed the dragon dropping beside us.

Eyes glazed with fear, the misfits crowded together. They covered their ears, trying to muffle the alarm.

I moaned; I knew too well what sorts of demons lurked near.

"Malcolm," my misfit father whispered.

I dropped my head, not wanting to look into his eyes. He seemed a demon to me as well. I wanted this night to end now!

But it was only beginning.

The bells stopped abruptly. In their place, real demon roars rose.

My body trembled, remembering last night. Remembering the blood. I bit my tongue before a scream left my mouth.

"Malcolm!" Somehow my father's voice cut through the deafening demon roars.

"No! Get away!" With a whimper, I pulled free of the mutant. But I couldn't stop from taking one last look. He was so much like I recalled yet so different. I pressed the shark tooth against my throat. My father wore the exact pendant around his neck. I groaned.

FROM the GRAVE

"I don't want a misfit father who's not even monster enough to stay dead." I wiped a claw across my eyes and turned toward the swamp. The deep black waters promised a quick conclusion to this night—one way or another.

"Wait. Don't jump!" cried my father.

I shook my head, but before I'd even lifted a hoof, thundering snarls rose behind us. We all whirled about.

A werewolf trio, with crazed eyes and foaming mouths, rounded the corner—heading straight for us. Their snarling lips curled back, revealing sharp, glistening teeth. Even though the bells had just rung, blood already dripped from their mouths. We would not be their first kill of the night. I shuddered, seeing once again the ancient gremlin's blood splattered across the cemetery.

The dragon rose stiffly into the air. The four of us remaining on the ground huddled near the water's edge.

With bloodthirsty growls, the creatures surrounded us on three sides. They crouched, ready to attack. My insides jelled. My limbs froze. Had the nearness to my misfit father zapped me of my monster wiles? Or was I not such a true-blood troll after all?

"Get down!" Frank yelled.

The mummy shoved my father into the muddy ground. Frank pulled me down with the others.

"Snotfargle!" I cried as my snout jammed into the muck. "Get your misfit hands off me!"

I dropped to all fours, scrambling on claws and hooves back toward the swamp. But my father caught one of my hooves and clamped down tight. More werewolves' growls stopped me. I glanced up. Our hairy attackers were still hunched low, but edging much closer.

"Use some of your fire, Frank!" said the mummy.

The stupid puss nuggets had gone zany with the attack. We had no fire.

My father's claw quivered on my leg. "No! Surrounded by these grasses, we could all die in the flames."

"I'd rather face a fire than the Demon Hours," Frank muttered.

The crazy misfit stood up. I swear I saw an *X* glowing in his hand. I snorted. What magic was this!

When the first of the werewolves jumped, Frank held his blue hand high. I could barely hear his whisper, "Granny, you gotta help it work this time." Then he took a deep breath and growled.

"Ratzbotchin!" I pulled back as a huge fiery blast shot from Frank's right palm.

The oily swamp grass erupted in flames. The lead werewolf couldn't divert his leap and landed in the inferno. He yelped and rolled, but to no avail. The flames soared higher. His body was quickly engulfed.

My eyes followed the other two. They whined and yipped but soon skirted the blaze. Their yips turned to snarls as they dared to tread along the far swamp edge toward us. I rubbed my claw across my open mouth and smeared the drool on my vest. Only crazed monster creatures would risk fire and water in order to kill their prey.

We too were edged in by the flames. I quivered. The swamp waters behind us were the only escape route.

"Watch out!" Frank called to the mummy.

"Too late," I muttered.

A trailing end of the mutant's wrapping hung too close to the fire. Soaked with embalming oils, the strip flared with a "pfffishht" and burst into flames. In a rush, the fire climbed up the strip toward the creep's half-wrapped body.

Whoooosh!

FROM the GRAVE

I shook some drops of water from my head, but the bulk of it had splashed over the mummy. The dragon gurgled as she hovered above. I held my claws over me as another big splash from the dragon cleared a small pathway. The mummy, clutching his strips tightly about him, was already threading his way through the flames.

Frank tried to push me and my father forward. "Go! We need to get to Granny's now!" He motioned with his head to the remaining two demon wolves, treading the water's edge, only a short distance away.

His big blue hands were firm. His eyes clear, intent. Almost monsterly. I grunted. Feeling truly defeated. "No!" I repeated. "I can't be saved by misfits." If I did, then I'd be the one who was more misfit than monster.

My father grabbed my shoulders. "We're all monsters, son. No misfits here."

I must have lost my balance then because I slid into his embrace. For a heartbeat, I let his arms wrap around me and his claws hold me tight. He was my dad and I was his son. True-blood trolls united.

A werewolf howled. My mind cleared. I spun about. They were nearly on top of us, as was the fire. I pushed away from my misfit father. My awful mutant father who I hated, hated, hated! I refused to be the son of a misfit. I'd rather die. And I'd not let these low-life creeps save me, Malcolm McNastee. No, I would end this night my way.

With a low growl, I held up my claw in a Junior Scare Patrol salute.

"Monster or die," I said. This time I didn't hesitate. With a leap, I dove into the black swamp.

CHAPTER TWENTY-FIVE

Monster Rule #13: Monster or die!

FRANK'S TALE

"Malcolm!" cried Mr. McNastee. But before he could take a step toward his son, the immense gray wolf leaped on Mr. McNastee's back. His bared teeth sunk into the older troll's shoulder.

Although my anger in the past had led to tragedies, I knew that now I must rely on my rage to fuel my strength and my resolve. "Arrrrgghh!" I screamed, welcoming the hot anger that boiled inside of me. Harnessing my fury, I shot a fiery blast at the attacking wolf.

The scent of scorched fur filled my nostrils. Before I could aid Mr. McNastee further, the second werewolf jumped at me. I ducked and caught the creature's underside. I catapulted the snarling demon into the swamp behind me. His flailing and yelping filled the air.

As Malcolm had said, "Monster or die!" I tried to find a clear shot at Mr. McNastee's attacker.

But both of them rolled in the tall grass. One on top and now the other. With a loud growl, McNastee lowered his head and gouged the werewolf in the throat with a horn. The creature cried out in pain and loosened its hold.

A whoosh of water cascaded down on the werewolf from Georgina hovering above. Her tired wings flapped weakly. Oliver sat atop her, unraveling strips.

Using all my Frankenstein might, I pulled Mr. McNastee free from the waterlogged werewolf. Then I shoved the creature back toward the fire. Flames snapped around it, blocking it in. I fired another blast from my hand. The wolf drew back, cringing from the heat surrounding him now on all sides.

"We're trapped too!" called Mr. McNastee.

It was true. The flames encircled us. We had nowhere to run—not even the swamp.

"Here!" yelled Oliver, tossing down strips to us. "Grab hold!"

With mighty jumps, we grabbed at the dangling strips, catching them just above the flames. Georgina grunted as we clutched the wrappings. But her wings flapped too weakly. We barely cleared the brush fire. Mr. McNastee yelped as the heat singed his legs, but my blue skin felt no pain.

Finally, we cleared the flames, still dangling from Oliver's wrappings.

"Woo hoo, Georgina!" Oliver yelled. "You did it."

"But . . . I can't make it much farther." Her raspy voice was nearly too weak to hear.

We'd almost made it back to Mushington Way when my strip tore. I tumbled to the ground. With a lame somersault—not at all graceful like Oliver—I rolled on my shoulder and landed in a clump of swamp grass. Mr. McNastee too, lost his grip and fell a short distance in front of me. I pushed myself up to go to him.

Georgina, already so terribly tired and banged up, totally lost balance. Oliver leaped off just before she crashed near the street.

I pulled Mr. McNastee to his feet. "Can you walk?"

He nodded. We stumbled to where Georgina lay. Oliver was fanning her with one of his strips.

Headlights blinded us from the left. A monstrous roar erupted on our right. A familiar bus screeched to a stop before us. On our other side, a giant Ogre, arms extended, mouth wide, lumbered quickly toward us.

Mr. Aldolfo flung open the doors of the O.M.O bus, slamming them directly into the Ogre's face. The attacking monster crumpled to the ground.

With a wink, our bus driver said, "You need a ride?"

Oliver and I tried to tie up the semi-conscious Ogre with mummy strips, while Mr. McNastee attempted to shove Georgina on the bus. We all barely made it on just before the Ogre shook off his blow to the head—and all of the wrappings.

Mr. Aldolfo banged shut the bus doors. The Ogre howled, pounding on the bus. One of the side windows shattered from the Ogre's blow. Mr. Aldolfo floored the accelerator and rolled the back tires over the Ogre's feet. Louder roars followed behind us. I glanced back and saw the Ogre limp away, but I spied the flick of a familiar-looking tail disappearing into a clump of jangleberry bushes as we passed. Mr. Aldolfo's voice pulled me away from the window.

"Lucky for all of you I ran late on my way home from the Shadowlands," Mr. Aldolfo said, hunching behind the wheel. "And that I headed home on Mushington Way."

"Yeah, lucky us," I said, fighting to catch my breath and calm my fury. "Thanks, Mr. Aldolfo." I turned to Georgina. "Are you okay?"

"That's . . . it . . . for me." Oliver caught Georgina's head in his lap before she fainted.

The bus lurched forward. "She probably just needs some water and rest," said Mr. Aldolfo. "Looks like you all have had quite the adventure."

I nodded. "Yeah, well, if you could drop us off at Granny's, I'm hoping the adventure's over with."

Our bus driver tipped his cap and floored the accelerator, skidding around the corner by Granny's house.

Mr. McNastee sat stooped beside me, rocking back and forth. "Malcolm . . . Malcolm . . ." he moaned.

My head sunk to my chest. We'd rescued Malcolm's father from Exxillium only to return him to this terrible tragedy. Whenever we'd studied compromised missions in our Monster Scare Tactics class, Ms. Hagmire always told us, "Keep calm and scary on." Much easier said than done in the real monster world.

Mr. Aldolfo breaked to a stop beside Granny's cellar door. He and I hurriedly helped Mr. McNastee down the steps to safety.

In the dim underground room, Zelda hobbled toward us, using the shovel as a crutch. Her torn hat sat atop her head. "I didn't know if you guys were gonna make it back or not. I didn't even dare try to see a vision."

"Not everyone made it back," I whispered, thinking of Malcolm.

Then Oliver, Mr. Aldolfo, and I managed to move a semi-awake Georgina downstairs as well.

A silent Mr. McNastee slumped over the table. I found the ingredients and Zelda mixed the potion for Georgina's clouded head. Mr. Aldolfo perched on the bottom step to wait until the Demon Hours ended before heading home. He promised to drop me and Oliver off on his way. Outside, muffled roars and howls still sounded.

In the murky dim, I studied the odd monsters surrounding me. Each had used their special skills this night. Without our teamwork, I doubted we could have survived.

I clasped my right hand in my left, tracing the softly glowing X. Granny's aid from the grave had kept me and the others alive this night. She had helped me face the demons of my world—both inside and out. But even though I'd finally proven to be more than monster enough, I couldn't tell anyone of my monsterly exploits—not without revealing my part in the Exxillium escape.

And what of Malcolm? Had he chosen death by drowning rather than admit to the world he had a misfit dad—or face the possibility that he was part misfit too?

Yeah, Malcolm was my sort-of enemy. Still, somehow I hoped he realized this night that he was monster enough. That we were all monster enough.

"Monster or die, Malcolm," I muttered. "Monster or die."

ACKNOWLEDGMENTS

A story starts as a tiny germ of an idea in an author's head and then blossoms into full awesomeness with the cultivating hands of many. The premise of this story—stuffed with zany creatures of every make and model—began with a simple idea: creatures deemed misfits would prove they are more than enough. My challenge was to make monsters entertaining and endearing while showing that truly every monster is special.

I had much help along the way to keep me in monster mode. First and foremost was my amazing husband who simply refused to let me give up when the demons of doubt threatened. He deserves a Frankenstein hug for all his encouragement.

Also major in making this happen were my family and friends, especially Matt and Jordan; Dan and Megan; mini-monsters Sam and Max; and of course my mom and dad and extended family who taught me all about monstrous love. And my special friend, Cindy. Thank you for your ongoing support. I am a lucky lady.

Thanks, as well, to my author friends and critique group colleagues who kept me heading in the right direction. A salutatory snap of a scaly tail to my talented St. Louis Children's Writers Group cohorts, to my encouraging SCBWI Mentor Vicki Erwin, and to my top-notch local retreat group partners Stephanie Bearce, Sue Bradford Edwards, Jeanie Ransom, Kristin Nitz, and teacher Darcy Pattison, who predicted that *From the Grave* would be published. And to the other Sweet Sixteeners, who joined hands with me on our debut ride and offered so much support.

Finally, I'd like to thank the artistic Jolly Fish Press team who brought my monsters to life in vivid and delightful color. And last but certainly not least, TJ da Roza, my editor who immediately fell in love with my crazy creatures. Without him, my monsters would still be haunting only my dreams. His invaluable insights for shaping the story into a frightfully fun read made all the difference. Thanks, TJ, for helping me keep calm and scary on!

Each of us is a unique combination of monster and misfit. In our own world, where too many are taught to fear and abhor what is different, I hope my monster story helps highlight the need for compassion rather than hatred—for acceptance rather than condemnation.

Monster On!

CYNTHIA REEG, an intrepid librarian, ventured from behind the book stacks to contend with quirky characters and delightful dilemmas in her very own picture books and middle grade novels. Her amazing husband, two grown sons, two adorable grandsons, and awesome family have aided Cynthia on this wild and wonderful adventure. While she has had her share of worldly adventures—fishing for piranhas in the Amazon, climbing the Great Wall of China, and white-water rafting in New Zealand—she's mainly a Midwestern girl. A Kansas native, she's also lived in Illinois, Oklahoma, Indiana, and Ohio. Currently she resides in St. Louis, Missouri, and loves to vacation in Florida and New Mexico. Cynthia enjoys tennis, hiking, reading, and hanging out with her family.

For more information, visit www.cynthiareeg.com.